WHAT HE DIDN'T TELL ME

JENNY LYNNE

D1520358

ISBN 9798853688261

To Andrea, Brenda, Brooke, Christina, Colleen, Deleah, Julie, Kasie, Kathy, Lois, Mandy, Sara, Sarah, and Shanna

Chapter One

"Have you ever wished a night could go on forever?"

I ask that question so softly that I'm not sure anyone heard me until Star whispers, "I think I wished that a million times tonight."

She's wedged up against me in the back seat of a limo. Both of us are wearing evening gowns—mine white lace and hers red satin—and we each have a tuxedo jacket draped over our bare shoulders. Dylan is sitting pressed up against my left side. Mateo is squeezed in on Star's right.

The four of us have been best friends since kindergarten. Tonight, we got together to celebrate my twenty-fifth birthday. They rented a limo, and we visited our childhood hangouts, reliving some of our favorite memories. We got a few strange looks, because we were incredibly overdressed for places like Mario's Pizza and Candy's Karaoke Bar, but I had the time of my life, eating and drinking and laughing and singing with the people who I love and who love me more than anything in the world. It's because of my best friends that my childhood is filled with happy memories. I'm not sure if I could have survived it without them.

Over the years, our friendship has undergone some changes. The biggest one happened about twelve years ago. Toward the beginning of seventh grade, I began to look at Dylan with different eyes. I started daydreaming about holding hands with him ... and kissing him. When I shared these thoughts with Star, she told me that she felt the same way about Mateo. But neither of us dared to tell the boys about our feelings, because we didn't want to hurt our friendship with them.

And then, one night, the four of us were at Dylan's house watching a movie. Halfway through the rom-com Star had chosen, she had to go to the bathroom. Mateo took that opportunity to go make more popcorn. That left Dylan and me on his couch, alone together.

I turned to him and blurted out, "I wish you were my boyfriend."

Without a word, he looked deep into my eyes. And then, Dylan leaned toward me, and we kissed for the first time. The kiss went on for a while, because neither of us wanted to stop.

When Star and Mateo finally came back to the living room, they were holding hands. I looked at their clasped hands and gave them a questioning look.

Mateo said, "Star and I saw you guys making out, so we went into the kitchen to give you some privacy."

Star nodded. "While we were waiting, I asked Mateo what he thought about you two getting together and he said ..."

"I wish it was us," Mateo finished.

Our friendships changed remarkably that night, but the changes felt incredibly right, as if we had slipped off a perfect outfit and traded it for one that fit us even better.

Now, I rest my head against Dylan's chest, and our fingers intertwine. In my reflection in the window glass, I see that the curls I forced into my sandy-brown hair are still cascading perfectly, the way hair normally does only in magazines. In the hazy reflection, I can almost see my childhood self ... a little girl on the cusp of becoming the woman she was meant to be. I haven't become that woman yet, but hopefully that's about to change.

Ever since I graduated from high school, I've been puttering around at jobs I hated while my friends pursued their passions. Dylan is already halfway through his internship as an architect, and Star and Mateo are almost finished with medical school. But, in a few months, I'll be starting my freshman year of college in New York City, where Dylan is doing his internship and Star and Mateo are going to med school. I'm about to start the adult life I always wanted with my three childhood best friends still by my side.

I glance at Dylan, and he smiles. Even though I've struggled a lot to find my place in the world, he has always been there for me. Accepting me without judgment. Never pushing me, but always wanting the best for me. He brushes my hair away from my eyes, and he moves in to kiss me.

I let my eyelids flutter closed—

Suddenly, there is a loud honk. My eyes spring open as the limo jerks to the right. A horrible screech of tires is followed by the sound of shattering glass. The limo hits something solid, and the ground slips out from under us. I look through the window and see that we are airborne over a body of water. My stomach rises into my chest as we crash into it, as if smashing into cement.

Murky water rushes fast into the limo. Horror floods my veins when I see Dylan lying crumpled on the floor. He's breathing, but when I shout his name, he doesn't stir. Star and Mateo are still in their seats, but their eyes are unfocused, as if they are in shock. Blood streams rapidly down Mateo's face from a large wound on his forehead.

I unbuckle my seatbelt and kneel down on the floor next to Dylan.

"Erin, are you okay?" Star asks me in a trembling voice.

I shake my head. "I'm fine, but Dylan isn't."

Star unfastens her seatbelt and kneels on the floor. Her shaky fingertips check him for a pulse, then she turns to me, her eyes distressed. "Keep his face above the water, but don't move his neck too much, in case his spine is injured."

"The doors and windows won't open," Mateo shouts.

I look over and see that he has released his seatbelt and is now moving about the limo. He kicks hard at the windows, but nothing happens.

"We need to find something we can use to shatter the glass," Star says.

The three of us yank open every compartment in the limo, but they hold only bottled water, bags of snacks, and napkins. The air pocket around us is getting smaller by the second. There's almost no air left to breathe. I kick at a window as hard as I can, while being careful to keep Dylan's mouth and nose above the rapidly rising water.

"I love you guys," I say through the tears trickling over my lips. "I need you to hear that one last time ... in case we don't make it out of this."

"We love you too ... more than anything," Mateo grunts, wiping the blood from his face, as he continues kicking at a window.

"Of course we do," Star says as she tries to use the heel of her shoe to break the glass. "But nobody here is dying any time soon."

Star has always been an optimist. She doesn't give up if there is even the slightest chance of success. She wants to be an ER doctor, and I know she would be an incredible one. She is amazingly adept at solving even the most difficult puzzles. But not every puzzle has a solution.

Mateo has memorized the names of every major nerve and blood vessel in the body, along with each of its branches. He wants to be a heart surgeon. When he was a kid, he used to take apart broken appliances and try to figure out what was wrong with them. Most of the time he was able to get them working again. I bet he'd be terrific at fixing broken hearts.

And Dylan …

Dylan and I were supposed to get married someday. He promised that, as soon as we could afford it, he was going to build us a house overlooking the ocean. I couldn't wait to live in that house, along with the kids we were definitely going to have and a cat or a dog or, more likely, both.

But now …

Our pocket of air is down to just a sliver.

Mateo takes a breath and drops underwater, still furiously trying to break the windows.

Star takes a desperate gulp of air, and I take one too.

Hold your breath, Dylan, I pray.

And then our faces are underwater.

I close my eyes, holding onto my last breath, knowing that, when I can't hold it anymore, I will drown.

Chapter Two

A hand touches my shoulder. Without releasing the breath I'm holding, I turn toward it. But all I see is darkness. Something is covering my eyes. I claw at my face, desperately trying to get it off ...

And then I do.

I take in my surroundings.

I'm not trapped inside a sinking limo. Not anymore.

I'm on an airplane, heading to Los Angeles, trying to escape the nightmares that have haunted me for the past three months, even when I'm awake.

A flight attendant peers down at me, his forehead furrowed. I guess I probably look as distraught as I feel. My stomach knots with embarrassment, and my gaze falls to my hands, where I'm clutching my pink satin eye mask as tightly as a drowning person clutches a life preserver.

"Miss, I need your seatback in the upright position in preparation for landing," the flight attendant says. His tone is gentle, the way people talk when they are speaking to someone fragile.

"Okay," I murmur, raising my seatback and shoving my eye mask into the pocket of my sweatpants.

Around me are staring eyes, but they look away before I make eye contact. I open the window shade and let my vision adjust to the bright sunlight reflecting off the tops of the puffy clouds below us. Even though I learned in physics how planes are able to fly, it never fails to amaze me that something so heavy can stay up in the sky just by continuing to move forward.

Suddenly, everything outside the window goes white. But only for a second. Then the world beneath the clouds is revealed. Tiny houses line serpentine streets. Many of the homes have a sparkling blue pool in the backyard. There are mountains in the distance. Los Angeles looks so different from New York. Maybe life will be different for me here. I need it to be.

The plane dips a few times and then hits the runway harder than it should. The woman sitting next to me gasps, but I don't. Ever since the accident, sensations have felt different than they used to. Either I am extra-sensitive to them or I feel numb. Right now, I feel numb.

Panels on the wings lift up to slow us down, and the plane fights against the air. I like this feeling because it's strong enough to cut through my deadened senses, if only for a few moments. I want to feel *something*. I want to feel like I'm still alive.

That's why I came to Los Angeles. The last time I was here, I was with Dylan, Star, and Mateo. In our senior year of high school, the four of us spent spring break camping on the living room floor of Star's aunt's Beverly Hills condo so we could spend our days visiting L.A.'s famous sights. It was our first vacation together— the first of many—and it was one of our favorites. I thought that, by coming back here, I could relive some of the happy memories of our trip and escape my pain. I don't know if that's possible, but I feel like I have to try.

As the plane slowly rolls toward the terminal, a woman's voice over the PA system officially welcomes us to Los Angeles. I keep my face turned toward the window even though there isn't much of interest outside. I don't want to look at the woman next to me. After seeing me wake up from my nightmare, I'm sure she is wondering if there is something wrong with me. I don't want her eyes to search my face, trying to figure me out. I don't want to risk having her ask me if I'm okay, because I don't want to tell her the answer: I'm not.

* * *

The airport shuttle van drops me off in the parking lot of a tired-looking motel. The place looked slightly better in the pictures online, but not much. The driver tosses my suitcase onto the concrete in front of me, and it promptly topples over. He doesn't bother to right it. I tip him anyway.

As I wheel my suitcase into the cramped motel office, the balding man behind the desk looks up and gives me a closed-lipped smile. "Checking in?"

"Yes," I say.

"I'm going to need to see your credit card and photo ID," he replies.

I hold out my driver's license. "The man who answered the phone told me I'd get a discount if I pay with cash."

"Erin Winters," he reads off my ID with a smirk as he plucks it from my hand.

Suddenly, I feel uncomfortable with the fact that I have just given this man my name and home address.

"It's eighty a night plus a two-night deposit," he tells me.

Over the phone, I was told that the cash rate would

be seventy-five dollars, but I don't argue. Eighty a night is still better than one hundred ten dollars per night, which was the second-best hotel rate I could find for the dates of my trip. I need to conserve money where I can. My practically-minimum-wage jobs over the years haven't left me with a whole lot of money in my bank account. I wish now that I'd taken Dylan up on his offer to move in with him, instead of spending most of my income renting crappy apartments. But not just because of the money. It would have given me more time with him. I thought I'd have plenty of time to spend with Dylan once I got my life together. I was wrong.

I pass the man two hundred forty dollars, and he hands me back my ID, along with a key attached to a mangled metal tag with the number "9" printed on it in chipped black paint.

"Stay as long as you like," he says, "but you need to pay each day by noon." Then the man stares at me without speaking for long enough that I figure he must be done with me.

"Thank you," I say to him, and I leave the office.

Room Nine is right next to the cloudy-green motel swimming pool. When I unlock my door, I'm met by the smell of stale cigarettes in my non-smoking room. There are so many stains on the dingy, brown carpet that it almost looks like it was designed that way. I pull my suitcase into the room and shut the door behind me.

I'm not sure if I feel safer inside the room or out of it. The man in the motel office certainly has a spare key to my room, and I would definitely feel unsafe with him in here with me. Unfortunately, I can't lock the deadbolt, because there isn't one. I can't fasten the door security chain, because the chain has been torn right out of the doorjamb. I shiver when I imagine how that might have happened. I wonder what my father would think if he knew I was staying at a place like this. I guess he probably wouldn't care.

I march back to the motel office, bringing my suitcase with me.

The man barely looks up as I approach his desk. "Checking in?" he asks.

"No," I say. "I was just here. I just checked in, but my room smells like smoke, the carpet is filthy, and the security chain is broken."

"Right," he says. "They're all like that." He places a dusty pine-tree-shaped air freshener on the counter. "This will help."

It takes a moment before I realize he's serious.

"I'll be checking out tomorrow," I tell him.

I wish I could check out right now, but first I have to

find another place to stay.

I leave the air freshener on the desk, and I storm out of the office. Despite my nap on the airplane, I'm completely exhausted. I just want to curl up in a ball and go to sleep, but I haven't eaten all day, and I shouldn't go to bed without eating something. I lock my suitcase inside my room and head back outside in search of food.

On the sidewalk in front of the motel, an expressionless woman wheels a blanket-draped stroller. A middle-aged man wearing jeans and a frayed t-shirt nods his head to the beat of the music blaring through his headphones. An older man with his hair in disarray picks through a trash can. He gingerly places a crushed plastic bottle into his bulging plastic bag before he walks on. I head in the opposite direction.

After a few minutes of walking, I sense the aroma of grilled onions. I follow it for more than a full block before I find the source: a food truck parked in a supermarket parking lot. The bean and cheese burrito is the least expensive item on the menu. I order that. The lone man inside the truck prepares the burrito as if he's done it thousands of times, and then he presents it to me.

I sit on one of the two plastic chairs beside the truck, open the foil wrapping of my burrito, and bite into the tortilla. The savory beans, melted cheese, and fresh salsa spill into my mouth, awakening my taste buds. For the next five minutes, I see nothing, hear nothing, and feel nothing other than the burrito I devour. Then I lick my lips clean and toss my crumpled foil into a trash can.

Feeling refreshed, I head into the supermarket and collect a box of store-brand breakfast bars, so that I'll have something to eat in the morning. On my way to the checkout area, I grab a pair of cheap flip-flops that I will wear, instead of going barefoot, in my motel room.

I choose the self-checkout lane, because I'd rather not interact with anyone, but the clerk at the 20-items-or-less lane waves me over. I force a smile and bring my basket to her.

"Did you find everything okay?" she asks as she scans my items.

"Yes," I say.

Since we're already talking, I ask her if she knows of anywhere around here where I can use the internet for free. I need to try to find a decent motel for the rest of my stay in Los Angeles. I can't imagine spending more than one night in the place where I'll be staying tonight. Honestly, I can't even imagine spending *one* night there, but I'm so tired that it feels like my only option.

"There's a public library on Franklin and Hillhurst." The woman draws a little map on the back of my receipt.

"I think it closes at six today, though."

The library isn't far from here, but it's almost six o'clock.

"That's okay," I say. "I'll go tomorrow."

When I exit the supermarket, I can't bear the thought of heading back to the motel just yet. I find myself drawn into a funky neighborhood of trendy clothing stores and atmospheric eateries. It's the kind of neighborhood that Dylan, Star, Mateo, and I sought out when we visited L.A.

A sweet, welcoming smell wafts from a tiny coffee shop. Having a cup of decaf in the evening usually helps me wind down before bed, so I head inside the shop. A few customers are scattered throughout the homey space. Everyone is alone, but not alone, preoccupied with their various electronic devices.

The cheery girl behind the counter smiles as I approach her. "What can I get for you?"

"A small decaf," I say.

"Anything else?"

"No, thank you." The fancy muffins and desserts are too expensive for my budget.

We exchange money, and then she asks, "What's your name?"

For an anxious moment, I think she's about to make

conversation, but then I notice her orange marker poised above a paper coffee cup. "Erin," I answer, holding my breath until she finishes scribbling down my name and turns away.

When she turns back, she hands me a warm cup of coffee. "Enjoy it, Erin. Cream and sugar are on the left."

I dump a few packets of sugar and plenty of cream into the coffee, then I choose a plush purple velvet chair that faces away from everyone else, plop down on the chair, and gaze out the window. Well-dressed people stroll along the sidewalk, mostly in groups or pairs. As I gaze at them, my vision blurs, and tears fall down my cheeks.

I don't know why I believed that coming back to Los Angeles might be able to ease my pain. Exploring L.A. with my best friends was fun, but they aren't here anymore, and they never will be again. Being here without them makes me feel more alone than ever before.

I sip my coffee until my tears abate enough that I can dry my eyes on my napkin, then I grab my supermarket bag and hurriedly head to the door. I just want to lock myself in my motel room and try to get enough sleep to face tomorrow.

As I deposit my cup in the wastebasket, I hear a

male voice say, "Excuse me."

I'm not sure whether he's talking to me, but even if he is, I don't care. I don't feel up to talking to anyone right now.

I keep walking.

A hand lightly touches my arm. I spin around and find myself facing a stranger who looks about my age. He's well-muscled, the kind of guy who could be intimidating if he wanted to be.

"I think you dropped something," he says, pointing to the purple chair where I was just sitting.

On the chair is a tiny dark-blue purse with glistening silver stars on it. It was a gift Star gave me for my twelfth birthday. I rush over to get it and exhale with relief when it is safely tucked back in my pocket. By the time I turn around again, the guy has returned to his laptop.

"Thank you," I say so quietly that he probably doesn't hear me.

And then I leave.

Chapter Three

Morning sunlight streams through holes in the saggy drapes, making my motel room appear even more pathetic than it did yesterday. The battered wooden table, chair, and nightstand are tightly wedged in a row between the door and the bed frame. I arranged this makeshift barricade last night, hoping it would be enough to keep someone from entering my room, or at least provide me with a warning if they tried to.

I slept fitfully, not enough to face the day, but I must face it anyway. A good thing about this room is that it's so unpleasant that leaving it to go out into the world is preferable to staying inside. I eat a breakfast bar, get dressed, and drag the furniture far enough away from the door that I can escape.

The air outside is cool. I yearn for the warmth of the

coffee shop I visited yesterday evening. I head north, back to the funky neighborhood, telling myself that today will be a good day. To start it off on the right foot, I will sit in the coffee shop and savor every drop of a nice cup of coffee, without crying. I'll even treat myself to a muffin.

And then a thought hits me: *I wonder if the guy who was there yesterday will be there again today.* That thought makes me anxious, although I'm not exactly sure why.

I arrive at the coffee shop and find it packed with people. The guy from yesterday *is* there, sitting at a table alone, typing on his laptop. His wavy brown hair hides his eyes from my view. Still, I am careful not to allow my gaze to rest on him. I don't want him to look up and catch me staring at him.

"What can I get you?" the girl behind the counter asks when I approach.

"A small regular coffee," I say. "And I'll also have a blueberry muffin."

"For here or to go?" she asks.

All of the chairs along the window are occupied, and there isn't even one empty table.

"To go," I reply.

Seconds later, I have my muffin—in a small paper

bag—and a coffee.

As I turn away from the counter, a familiar voice says, "You can sit here if you want."

It's *him*.

My gaze meets his, and he smiles warmly. He seems nice, but I'd rather not sit with a stranger. I decide to tell him that I can't stay, but for some inexplicable reason, I find myself muttering a thank you and depositing my muffin on his table.

I take my coffee to the cream and sugar station, and I look back at my tablemate. His fingers move rhythmically over the keys of his laptop, almost like he's playing a musical instrument rather than typing words into a computer. He's wearing unassuming brown pants that hang loosely over his long legs and a threadbare t-shirt.

I return to his table and quietly set down my coffee cup, trying not to disturb him. He doesn't seem to notice that I've joined him. *I guess he's not expecting a conversation.* I take a sip of my coffee and pop a piece of muffin into my mouth, squishing a large juicy blueberry with my tongue.

Suddenly, the guy closes his laptop. He stares at it for a moment, as if awakening from a trance, and then looks at me and asks, "Are you new to L.A.?"

I hastily swallow the food in my mouth. "I'm just visiting."

"How long are you visiting for?"

I feel my shoulders tighten. "I leave in four days. My college orientation is next week."

He exhales. "My school starts up next week too."

"You're in college?" I ask.

"Law school," he says.

"*You're* going to be a lawyer?" He doesn't look like the lawyer type. He's too artsy.

"Law school wasn't my idea," he says. "It was my father's."

"What did you want to do instead?" I ask him.

"I love creative writing," he says. "But it's tough to make money like that."

"Money isn't everything," I say.

"It isn't," he agrees. "So, why'd you come to Los Angeles?"

"I wanted to figure out if life is still worth living." I admit.

The guy searches my face. I think he's waiting for me to say that I'm just kidding. But I don't.

Finally, he says, "This is becoming an unusually deep conversation considering that we haven't formally introduced ourselves."

"I'm Erin," I say, giving him a small wave.

"I'm Ben," he says, waving back with a smile.

As I gaze into his eyes, I realize that I like Ben. I think, if we got to know each other, he and I could be friends. And that thought absolutely terrifies me.

I grab what's left of my muffin and coffee, and I rise to my feet. "I have to go."

Ben's forehead wrinkles with confusion. "Well ... I hope to see you again, Erin."

I try to convince myself that it would be okay to sit and talk with Ben a little more. But, no matter how hard I try, I can't.

"I'm sorry that I have to go," I say, and I walk out the door.

* * *

"I thought you were checking out today," the man behind the motel office desk says, barely hiding his characteristic smirk.

"I'd like to stay," I say. The truth is, even after spending over two hours on a library computer searching for last-minute hotel deals and making a ton of phone calls, this place still seems like my best option. Everything else is either too expensive or poorly located.

I hand over eighty dollars.

"Enjoy your day!" The man smiles broadly and, for the first time, I notice that some of his teeth have been sharpened into points, like fangs.

"Thank you," I mumble, swallowing my horror, and I leave the office.

I walk away from the motel, turn north, and head toward Griffith Observatory.

The observatory sits high on a hill overlooking Hollywood. Dylan, Star, Mateo, and I visited it on the first day of our trip to L.A. I'm not sure if I'm prepared to face the observatory yet or ever, but I don't give myself the opportunity to reconsider. I focus every bit of my energy into my footsteps, trying not to allow myself to think at all.

* * *

I'm sweating by the time I arrive at the edge of the expansive observatory lawn. Families with young children picnic on blankets set on the bright-green grass. A gray-haired couple poses for a photo. A slightly younger man and woman stroll past me, holding hands. As I approach the entrance to the imposing observatory building, my skin prickles with unease, but I ignore my apprehension and pull open the heavy door.

Inside is a vaulted atrium, its ceiling adorned with

fanciful images of people and animals against a backdrop of blue sky. When I saw it on my last visit, I found it intriguing, like something pulled from a vivid dream. But now looking up at the brightly painted ceiling makes me feel so lightheaded that I need to lean against the wall in the center of the room for support.

On the other side of the wall is a circular pit where a bronze pendulum swings back and forth. I watch the gentle swinging—trying to let it calm me—until the rod at the bottom of the pendulum hits one of the pegs in its path and the peg topples over. A docent is explaining how the pendulum works, but I don't listen. My preoccupied mind can't seem to focus on her words.

When I turn away from the pit, the atrium is bustling with people, and they seem to multiply by the second, until they block every exit. The echoing noise of their chatter rings in my ears. My heart speeds as my vision falters. I stumble to the perimeter of the room and sit down on the floor, my back pressed against the cold wall. Then I force myself to breathe, counting in my head as I inhale and exhale, the way my therapist taught me to do: *One Mississippi, Two Mississippi, Three Mississippi. Three Mississippi, Two Mississippi, One Mississippi.* Then I force myself to rise to my feet.

I let go of the wall and start down the corridor on the

left, trying to direct my attention to the exhibits. During our visit, Star absolutely adored these exhibits, and her enthusiasm was contagious. Watching her take in this place was like seeing a kid take in Disneyland for the first time.

Now, as I walk the disconcertingly narrow corridor, it's all I can do not to run as fast as I can to the nearest exit. Ever since the accident, I often get overwhelmed by feelings of claustrophobia. I guess that's understandable, given that I was trapped underwater inside a sinking limousine, certain I was about to die, but I hate living like this. After I escaped death, I was thrust into a painful new world. A world that's getting harder and harder to inhabit. I think the only way to get past my fears is to face them. The thing is, I don't know if I can.

Suddenly, over the PA system, a man announces something about a demonstration of the Tesla coil. All at once, people surge into the corridor, completely blocking my path.

I press my back against the nearest wall and stare at the Tesla coil—a monstrous metal thing in the center of a wire cage, behind a pane of glass. I tell myself to calm down as I count in my head, *One Mississippi, Two Mississippi, Three Mississippi. Three Mississippi, Two Mississippi ...*

Without warning, lightning bolts surge from the coil. The crowd murmurs with delight and moves toward the glass, leaving an empty space in front of me. I peel myself from the wall and race to the end of the corridor, where there is a door marked "Exit." I slip through it and step into the warm sunlight. After a few minutes of standing practically immobile, the tightness in my chest subsides enough that I feel capable of continuing on.

I climb a staircase leading to the grand walkway that runs across the front of the observatory building. My friends and I spent nearly an hour on this walkway, admiring the views of Griffith Park and posing for photos. I find the precise spot where we threw our arms around each other and turned toward the camera, wearing our goofiest smiles. That picture was the wallpaper on my phone until it became too painful to look at.

As I stand where my friends and I once stood, sadness envelops me like a suffocating fog. I try to remember what it felt like to be happy here with them, but when I attempt to picture their smiling faces, the images fade into memories that will haunt me as long as I live. I see Mateo lying motionless on a bed of gravel and shattered glass, his face streaked with blood. And Dylan laid out lifeless on a broken slab of concrete. And Star with her head slumped to one side, her eyes open, and her soul gone.

Chapter Four

I toss the cellophane that once held a tuna sandwich from the Café at the End of the Universe into a Griffith Observatory trash can. I bought that sandwich mostly because it was past dinnertime and I hadn't eaten anything since breakfast. I ate it without enjoyment, even though the last time I was here Dylan and I both declared the tuna sandwiches the best we had ever tasted.

I should probably do a preemptive pee and head back to my motel now. I want to get there before the sun sets. I don't want to be walking around in the dark alone.

Searching for the restrooms, I push open an opaque glass door and discover a massive two-level underground chamber that I didn't know existed. Tremendous photos of stars cover one wall, and an impressive model of the solar system graces the lower level. A pang of regret tightens my throat as a thought enters my brain, *Star would have loved this place.*

As I walk through the upper level of the chamber, I glance at the meteors displayed in glass cases along the wall. They look so much like ordinary rocks that it's hard to believe they came from outer space. Back when those meteors were lying on the ground somewhere after having fallen from the sky, I bet people walked right past them, never realizing how special they were.

After I locate the restrooms and pee, I descend a staircase that leads to the lower level of the chamber. Boisterous children are running about, playing with scales designed to tell people what they would weigh on different planets. I take refuge in a quiet alcove with a large drum labeled "Seismograph." As I study its readouts from various earthquakes, something large lands on the floor behind me. I spin around and see not some*thing*, but some*one*: a little girl, maybe five years old. The wispy, golden curls in her hair bounce adorably.

"Did I scare you?" she asks me softly.

"No," I say, my heart still pounding. "You startled me."

"I'm sorry," she says, her eyes remorseful.

I offer her a smile. "It's okay. I'm fine."

"Hey!" she says, pointing at the seismograph drum.

"We made an earthquake!"

I look at the drum, and I'm surprised to see a small blip from just seconds ago. Bewildered, I read the description next to the display. And then I understand. Apparently, this drum measures vibrations from a sensor located in the floor.

I point to the tile below us and tell the girl, "There's a sensor under there."

Her eyes widen with excitement. She jumps and then checks the seismograph, but the needle doesn't move. She's just too small.

"Why don't we do it together?" I suggest.

"Good idea!" she exclaims. "Ready? Three, two, one, blastoff!"

We jump.

She checks the seismograph and then bounces with joy. "That was COLOSSAL! Let's do it again!"

I smile. "Okay."

"Three, two, one, blastoff!" she shouts.

We jump and she giggles. I laugh too.

I haven't laughed since the night of my birthday ... before the accident.

"Eliza!" A frazzled woman pulls the little girl away from me. "How many times have I told you not to bother people?"

The girl lowers her head. "Sorry, Mommy."

"She wasn't bothering me," I say to the woman. "She's a great kid."

"Thank you," the woman says coldly, then she turns back to the girl. "Time to go."

Eliza gives me a forlorn look. "Bye, nice lady."

I mask my sadness with a smile. "Bye, Eliza."

I watch the two of them walk away until they disappear into the crowd, then I crumple onto a bench, feeling suddenly drained. In a time that feels like it was long ago, I wanted to be a kindergarten teacher. I imagined having students like Eliza, spunky and curious. The thought of inspiring children to learn new things once excited me. Maybe it still does a little.

I glance at my watch, and panic rises into my throat. It's getting late. The sun will be setting soon. I sprint upstairs and dash outside. The sky is pink and purple, and it's beginning to darken. I hurry to the hiking trail that I used earlier today, and I descend toward Hollywood, passing through shadows cast by trees in the fading light. As I round a bend, I spot a skinny dog standing in the center of the path. When I stop short, he turns to look in my direction, and my heart accelerates with fear. *He's not a dog. He's a coyote.*

Behind me, I hear movement in the bushes. I glance

back and see two more coyotes creeping toward me. There might be more, hiding in the shadows, but even if there aren't, I'm already outnumbered. *I'm trapped.*

"GO AWAY!" I yell at the coyotes.

The animals stare at me with predatory eyes.

"GO AWAAAAAAAY!" I shout again, my voice faltering.

Instead of sounding strong, I sound weak and broken.

All alone like this, I am easy prey.

My breaths become uneven, and tears fill my eyes.

I hate being weak. I hate being broken.

I hate being alone.

I hate that my best friends are dead, and I'm still here.

WHY AM I STILL HERE?

Pain erupts from me in a guttural wail aimed at the stars. The coyotes bound off into the darkness, but I continue screaming. Not at the coyotes. At the pain that won't lessen no matter how hard I cry. At the fear that it will never leave me. That it will keep eating away at me until I die. I traveled all the way from New York to Los Angeles in a desperate attempt to escape my pain, but it's here too. Because it's inside me. And you can't escape what's inside you.

Sobbing harder than I ever have before, I take off running. The air stings my tear-drenched cheeks. My throat throbs. My shins ache ...

And the longer I run, the more unbearable the pain grows.

* * *

When I reach the funky neighborhood where I had coffee this morning, I finally stop running. I wipe my face dry before I walk past the lighted windows of the shops and restaurants. At one particularly inviting café, friends and couples dine outdoors under twinkling white lights. The sandwiches make my mouth water. It might be a good idea to have something more to eat today, but I think it would break my heart to sit here at a table all alone.

A few windows away, the coffee shop is buzzing with activity. My purple velvet chair is currently occupied by two people, even though it's meant for only one, but I hardly register them. I'm busy looking for someone else. For Ben. And then I see him, sitting at a table, typing away at his laptop with the intensity of someone who is writing a masterpiece. I hope he is.

Suddenly, my foot slips on the pavement, and my elbow bangs against the glass. Ben glances up from his work. I dart away from the window before he sees me—I think—and I start running again. I don't stop until I arrive at my motel room door.

I rush inside the room, lock the door behind me, and rebuild my barricade with the table, chair, and nightstand. Then I pull off my dirty clothes, and naked, except for flip-flops, I step under the shower's feeble drizzle, knowing that no matter how hard I try, it will be impossible to wash away my failure of a day.

Chapter Five

I barely slept last night. But at least I didn't have any nightmares that I can remember. Maybe all the exercise I got yesterday left me too tired to dream.

I climb out of bed, eat a breakfast bar, wash up, and get dressed. Then I stuff some cash into a waterproof wallet, toss a towel into my grocery bag, and burst out of my motel room, leaving it behind as fast as I can. Before I head off to my destination for today, I decide to make a quick detour to the coffee shop, mostly because I want to see Ben.

I'm not sure if I'd dare to ask if I can join him again at his table, or if I'd even dare say anything to him at all. And it's possible that he won't make any attempts to interact with me. The first time I saw him, he was being kind by letting me know I'd left my purse behind.

Yesterday, he offered me a seat because all of the other tables were occupied. This morning, it's a bit earlier in the day. The place might not be as busy. If there are plenty of unoccupied tables, Ben might just ignore me. But even if we don't interact at all, I still want to see him.

As I open the door to the coffee shop, my stomach sinks. It is much less crowded than it was yesterday morning. There are plenty of unoccupied tables.

And Ben isn't here.

At the counter, the same girl who took my order yesterday asks me, "What can I get you?"

"A small regular coffee," I say.

"Blueberry muffin?" she asks, remembering my order from yesterday.

I shake my head. "Not today."

"For here or to go?" she asks.

"For here," I say.

Moments later, I am presented with my coffee. I swirl in some cream and sugar, and then I reclaim my purple seat by the window. As I sip my coffee, I look out at the sidewalk ... hoping to see Ben, but by the time I finish, he hasn't arrived.

I can't help feeling deflated as I head on my way.

It takes about an hour for the public bus to get me from Hollywood to Santa Monica. After a short walk from where the bus drops me off, I stand where pavement meets sand, staring at the Pacific Ocean. When my friends and I arrived at this same spot years ago, Dylan and I yanked off our shoes and sunk our bare feet into the sun-drenched sand. Star and Mateo immediately followed suit. Then the four of us took off running, laughing as we raced toward the ocean. Now, I have to force myself to pull off my sneakers and socks and press my feet into the warm sand. Then I run, chasing the haunting memory of my friends' laughter toward the water.

When I'm close to the groups of families that dot the transition from dry sand to wet, I slow to a walk and look for a place to set down my things. I end up laying my bag and sneakers a few feet from a crumbling sandcastle. A toddler—who had been filling a moat around the castle with water—dashes toward the ocean with his empty bucket, squealing with delight. His mother acknowledges me with a hasty glance and then returns her attention to her phone.

I remove the t-shirt and shorts that cover my swimsuit, pull my swim goggles down over my eyes, and start toward the ocean, feeling uneasy. The wet sand is cold beneath my feet. The water must be colder. I don't allow myself to hesitate though. I walk into the water, resigned, and an icy wave crashes against my legs, splashing all the way up to my thighs. I shake away the chill and march ahead as the waves continue to smash against me. Higher and higher.

I take a breath and dive under the waves, trying to feel the joy that I felt when my friends and I swam around here like dolphins, exploring the depths of the ocean, stopping only to come up for air. That day, the underwater visibility was extremely good. Even in deep water, we could see all the way to the ocean floor. Today, the water is cloudy, and there are strands of kelp everywhere. Each time one whips against my body, my heart accelerates with fear. I feel like I'm in some kind of underwater horror movie, and it is only a matter of time before I meet my inevitable demise.

I turn back toward the shore, diving under a massive mound of kelp as I go. The snarled green tendrils undulate in the water, as if beckoning me. As I move away from them, something catches my eye ...

There is a large object tangled in the kelp.

No, it's not an object. It's a person ... a girl ...

It's *Star.* Her face looks terrified, as if she is

screaming a silent scream, but her open eyes are lifeless.

I gasp and suck in water. In a panic, I search for the quickest route to the surface, but all I see above me is an impenetrable blanket of kelp. I need air, but I can't get to it. And then something hits me from behind and yanks me backward. I try to pull away from it, but I can't break free. I am dragged deeper underwater. Away from Star. And away from the surface. My lungs beg for oxygen, but my body is too weak to fight for it. I close my eyes, certain, for the second time in my life, that I am about to die. This time, I feel ready.

All of a sudden, I sense air against my lips. I cough and sputter. A woman speaks into my ear in a soothing tone, but I can't make sense of what she's saying.

Then I feel my feet make contact with sand. I crawl onto it on my hands and knees.

"Are you able to walk?" the woman beside me asks.

I push her away before I vomit a stomachful of water into the surf.

And then I collapse.

* * *

A crinkly blanket covers my body. Fast electronic beeps speed up and slow down every time I take a shaky breath. I squint my eyes closed. The sunlight is too bright.

And then a shadow passes over me. Tentatively, I open my eyes.

"How are you feeling?" a man asks me.

He's wearing a uniform and a paramedic badge. Even though he is clearly here to help me, I feel an overwhelming need to escape.

I pull the oxygen mask off my face and force myself upright. As I do, I hear a wave break with a thunderous clap, and my head spins toward the ocean.

"We need to keep that oxygen on you for now," the man says to me, but I ignore him.

Out in the water, a female lifeguard—possibly the same woman who rescued me—is swimming toward the shore. She's dragging something with her. A second lifeguard meets her with a silver blanket, just like the one draped over me. He quickly covers the large object with the blanket, but not before I catch a glimpse of it. *It's the girl I saw in the ocean.*

That girl looked exactly like Star, but it can't be her. Star is buried in a cemetery in New York. I know in my head that it isn't Star under that blanket, but I need to prove it to my heart.

I pull off the wires attached to the stickers on my chest and make my way to the lifeguards, astonished that

I have the strength to walk. As I approach the female lifeguard, she moves in front of me, blocking my path to the girl.

"I need to see what's under that blanket," I say to her.

She shakes her head, her short blonde hair dripping water onto her shoulders. "Sorry. No."

I swallow hard, tears pricking my eyes. "When I was out in the ocean, I saw a girl tangled up in the kelp. I need to know who she was."

The lifeguard presses her lips together. "We think she's the girl who got caught in a rip current off Venice Beach two days ago."

"I need to see her again," I say, my eyes fixed on the blanket.

"Why?" the lifeguard asks.

"I just … *need* to." *I need to see that she isn't Star.*

"There are some things you can't unsee, as much as you wish you could," she says.

I understand exactly what she means, but I can't leave this beach without proving to myself that Star isn't here.

"Please," I beg the woman.

She inhales deeply and then takes a small step to the side. "If you feel this is something you need to do, for closure or whatever, I won't stop you."

I drop to my knees next to the blanket and lift one corner.

Chapter Six

The girl under the blanket isn't Star. She doesn't look anything like her. She doesn't even look like a person. Her body is bloated and purple. Her eyes are opaque. Her long brown hair is matted in knots. But her torn swimsuit has smiling cartoon flowers printed all over it, and her fingernails are painted light blue with a little pink heart on each one, reminders that this body once belonged to someone who had thoughts and feelings and dreams, like Star and Dylan and Mateo. Like them, her life was cut far too short.

Tears fall down my cheeks as I lower the blanket back to the sand. The lifeguard was right—the image of that girl will never leave my mind. It will join all the other horrible memories that have taken up permanent residence there.

"Thank you for letting me see her," I murmur to the lifeguard, who is now standing by my side.

"I hope that gave you what you needed." Her gaze searches my face, as if looking for the answer.

"It did," I assure her, but her forehead furrows with uncertainty.

Before I go, I ask, "Are you the one who rescued me from the water?"

She nods without speaking.

"Thank you for saving my life," I say.

But to be honest, I'm not sure if I'm glad that she did.

The crowd of onlookers parts for me as I walk off in search of my belongings. I quickly spot the little boy with the sandcastle. He's now sailing a toy boat in the castle moat, oblivious to the dead girl lying on the sand about fifty feet away. I can tell by the look of unease on his mother's face that she is painfully aware of the girl.

She cocks her head toward the blanket-covered body. "Is that the girl who drowned at Venice Beach the other day?"

"I don't know," I respond.

"You didn't see the story on the news?" she persists.

I stare at the ocean. "No."

The woman types something into her phone and,

after a few taps, hands it to me. On the screen is a photo of a girl with childlike eyes. Her long brown hair is pulled neatly back from her face. Words below the picture hit me like punches: "twenty-one years old" "pre-med student" "pushed her sister toward shore before she submerged." There's another photo below the story: the last photo taken of the girl. Her swimsuit is heart-wrenchingly familiar, with its smiling cartoon flowers. Although the girl in the photo hardly resembles the body lying in the sand, I know now that they are the same person.

As I hand back the phone, I notice a man lugging a news camera, picking his way through the sand, heading toward us.

"Looks like you're going to be famous!" the woman bursts out, as if it would be exciting to be on TV recounting what it was like to find a girl's dead body in the ocean.

"Not if I can help it." I yank my shirt and shorts over my damp bathing suit, stuff my towel and sneakers into my bag, and then I run.

* * *

I once heard that the easiest place to disappear is in a crowd, so I sprint toward Santa Monica Pier. Dylan, Star,

Mateo, and I spent an afternoon there, dancing to the invigorating music, taking in the ocean views, and eating way too much cotton candy. As the day wound down, we bought burgers, which we relished as we sat together on a bench and watched a fiery sunset over the ocean. After that, we took a twilight ride on the Ferris wheel, which was nerve-wracking for me, since I am not a fan of heights. As we ascended, Dylan let me squeeze one of his hands and Star let me squeeze one of hers, and Mateo whispered encouraging words to me until I was brave enough to open my eyes to take in the magical view of the darkening ocean and mountains beyond the twinkling lights of Santa Monica.

Now, I weave myself into the suffocating throng of people on the pier. The sounds and smells that were once exhilarating now assault my senses: grilling meat, chattering voices, hip-hop music. I wish I could quiet all of it.

At the end of the pier, I duck inside the ladies' room and rinse the lingering taste of vomit from my mouth. I smooth my hair into a ponytail, put on my sunglasses, and head back outside.

I'm feeling a bit lightheaded. Maybe I should try having something to eat. Not far from the restroom is the place where my friends and I bought our burgers. I join the queue.

"Next," a man shouts at me from one of the windows.

I hurry over to him and place my order, "A California veggie burger and a cup of ice water."

Moments later, I have a tray of food and no idea where to go with it. There aren't any unoccupied tables, and a sleeping man in ragged clothes occupies the bench where my friends and I sat the last time I was here.

I walk until I'm behind a slatted fence, in an area that I'm sure isn't meant for the public. I sit down on a plastic crate, balance my tray in my lap, and take a tentative bite of my burger. The seasoned veggies mix with the avocado and cheese, and memories of the last time I had this burger flood into me. Memories of a time when life seemed as if it could go on forever. Of a time when I believed that, for as long as I lived, I'd have my best friends by my side.

Tears start down my cheeks. I close my eyes and take bite after bite of my burger, until it's gone.

* * *

I walk as fast as I can along the firm wet sand, staying far enough away from the ocean that its waves can't reach me. Once Santa Monica Pier is far behind me, I trudge up the beach, toward the T-shirt shops and beachside restaurants that line the boardwalk. Then I put on my socks and sneakers and amble along the pavement, glancing up every intersecting street I encounter, trying to find one that looks familiar. Unable to spot anything that I recognize, I ask a woman whose sun-bleached hair makes me think that she might be a local, "Do you know how to get to the Venice Canals?"

"Head up Venice Boulevard and look for the sign on the right," she says.

A few intersections later, I turn up Venice Boulevard and feel a reassuring sense of déjà vu. Soon, I encounter the weathered sign that Dylan, Star, Mateo, and I followed to a hidden neighborhood of homes along picture-perfect canals. I walk along a small street until I finally spot some of the bungalows and skinny mansions that line the charming waterways. Their backyards and a narrow public walkway separate the houses from the water. Rowboats and kayaks are tied to miniature docks on the canal.

When we visited these canals, Star said that, if she lived in one of these homes, she would start every day by going kayaking. She and Mateo were planning to move to Los Angeles someday, maybe once they grew old and retired. They both agreed that Venice would be a perfect neighborhood to settle in. I think the two of them would have been incredibly happy here.

A group of ducklings and their mother clatter onto the walkway ahead of me. I pause to allow them to make their way unhurried into the water. The house beside the walkway is covered in layer upon layer of blossoming vegetation, making it look like something straight out of a fairy tale. Pink and purple flowers have engulfed the fence and grown up over the gate, partially hiding a mural of the canal. The painting seems to be almost a mirror image of what's behind me. The main difference is that most of the real-life homes are somewhat different from the ones in the mural. One home has a different paint job. One home is an entirely different structure. I move the flowers aside to get a better look at the mural.

"Can I help you?" a man says from the other side of the fence.

I shouldn't have touched the flowers. I'm about to let them fall back into place, when something stops me ...

On the just-uncovered part of the mural are two girls, one with wavy brown hair and one with straight blonde hair. My skin tingles with recognition.

"Your mural is beautiful," I say to the man.

He stands up, allowing me to get a look at him. His

gray hair is somewhat mussed, as if maybe he had been sleeping.

"Thanks," he says with a tinge of pride. "My mom painted it."

I point to the girls in the mural. "Do you know who those girls are?"

He shrugs. "Just some girls she saw here one day."

"I think that … one of them might be me." I take a breath to steady my voice. "And I think the other one is my friend, Star."

The man shakes his head dismissively. "Nope. My mom painted that mural probably thirty years ago."

I swallow my disappointment and look back at the mural with new eyes. When I do, I notice that the brown-haired girl is taller than the blonde one. Star is … was … taller than me. Of course, those girls aren't Star and me.

"I'm sorry I disturbed you," I say to the man.

"No worries," he says.

The ducks have waddled off the walkway and are now swimming in the canal, but I turn away from the direction that I was headed, and I start back the way I came.

* * *

As I walk along the beach, making my way back to Santa

Monica, I watch the ocean waves, half-expecting that they will leap up at any moment and drag me to my death. I wish they would. I'm tired of painful memories. I'm tired of nightmares. I'm tired of feeling sad all the time. I'm just ... tired of everything.

I stop and stare at the ocean. I ask if it will take me if I let it, and I wait in silence to see if it will answer. Far from shore, pelicans bob on the undulating water. Past them, a seabird plunges into the ocean with a splash. Further away, a dolphin arches out of the water and then dives back under. Another dolphin appears, just behind the first one, before vanishing again. Moments later, the two dolphins surface side by side. They disappear and then resurface, again and again. They seem to be together. Maybe they're friends.

And then I realize what I need to do if I am going to survive.

* * *

The bus from Santa Monica to Hollywood drops me off just steps from my motel, but I rush past it, hardly acknowledging it with a glance. I dodge pedestrians on the busy sidewalks, and I race all the way to the coffee shop.

There are only a few people inside. I wasn't sure if

Ben would be here, but he is, sitting at a table by himself, typing away on his laptop. My heart beats hard and fast as I enter the coffee shop, march over to Ben's table, and sit down. He stops typing and looks up at me expectantly.

I had thought I'd figured out exactly what I was going to say, but now I can't remember any of it.

Finally, I ask, "What were you typing?"

"A screenplay."

"What's it about?" I ask.

He shakes his head. "I don't know."

"How can you not know what it's about?" I ask, confused.

He sighs. "I can't figure out what to write."

"But you were typing so fast," I counter.

He turns his computer screen toward me. On it I read:

BOY

Hi.

GIRL

Hello.

And then those four words repeat, exactly in that order, over and over again. I scroll back a few pages, but I find only those four words.

"All this time, *that's* what you've been typing?" I ask.

Ben's gaze falls to the table. "I haven't even settled on the characters' names yet."

"But I thought you loved writing."

He exhales. "I have all these stories swimming around in my brain, but every time I try to start writing one of them, my mind goes blank. They say if you don't know what to write, then you should go ahead and write anything, and eventually a story will come. So far that hasn't worked."

"How long have you been at it?" I ask.

"Too long." Ben closes his laptop. "But enough about that. How are you enjoying L.A.?"

My eyes dampen. "I'm not."

His eyes flash with concern. "Did something happen to you?"

"This morning, I went for a swim at the beach, and I found a dead body in the water." The image of the girl's knotted hair and lifeless eyes surges into my mind, tightening my throat.

Ben looks at me with the same look that strangers have been giving me a lot lately, a look that makes me feel like they think I'm insane.

"It was the girl who disappeared two days ago at Venice Beach," I say defensively.

"Right," he says. "I heard about her."

I continue, feeling less defensive, "When I saw her under the water, I freaked out and nearly drowned. If the lifeguard hadn't rescued me, I probably would have died."

"I'm glad you didn't die," he says.

I lower my head without saying anything in response.

"Do you want to go for a walk?" Ben asks.

Maybe I should hesitate, but I don't.

Chapter Seven

Ben and I have spent the past several hours wandering around a sleepy neighborhood of twisting roads lined with tall trees, manicured lawns, and gorgeous mansions. We pass the time sharing happy stories about our childhoods. I don't tell Ben that most of the people in my stories are now dead.

As the sky begins to darken, Ben leads me back toward the coffee shop. It looks like our time together is drawing to a close, but I wish it wouldn't end.

We stroll past the patio of a restaurant, where a waiter is lighting the candles on the tables, now that day is drifting into night, and my stomach rumbles loudly.

"Hungry?" Ben asks me.

"A little," I admit.

His eyes brighten. "Follow me."

Ben races down the block so fast that I have to run to keep up with him. He stops right in front of the inviting café that I'd noticed last night but didn't want to go to all alone.

"Do you want to eat here?" he asks.

A smile spreads across my face. "I would love to."

* * *

"But I was actually wearing *ladies' pajamas*," Ben says, finishing yet another captivating story from his childhood.

As I picture Ben standing on stage singing his heart out in front of everyone at his high school, wearing baby-blue silk pajamas, I laugh. I can't help myself.

"All of your stories are amazing," I tell him. "Your screenplay is going to be incredible."

"I didn't make those stories up," Ben says. "Those things actually happened."

"Then maybe your screenplay should be based on a true story," I suggest.

Ben inhales thoughtfully and then says, "Yeah, maybe."

I lean back into my chair and take in the atmosphere of the café patio one final time. Our table is tucked between two trees with branches draped in the tiniest of lights. Before me is the only remnant of my dinner: an empty box that once contained a sandwich overflowing with crisp fresh vegetables, hummus, avocado, and crumbles of feta cheese.

The sandwich was delicious, but what I enjoyed most about this meal was Ben's company. Even when neither of us had anything to say, I felt surprisingly at ease with him. It seems impossible to be this comfortable with someone who is more or less a stranger, but somehow, I am.

* * *

After dinner, Ben insists on walking me back to my motel, and I accept, because I want to spend a bit more time together. But as my motel comes into view, I am eager to say our goodbyes. I don't want Ben to see how sorry-looking it is.

"I can walk the rest of the way by myself," I tell him.

Ben's forehead furrows, as he stops walking. "Okay."

"Will you be at the coffee shop tomorrow?" I ask him, hopeful.

He nods. "I'll be there with my laptop, trying to figure out how to write a screenplay."

Ben looks down at the sidewalk, suddenly appearing intensely sad. I wish I could make his sadness go away, like he's done for mine for the past several hours.

"Maybe you're trying too hard," I say. "Maybe you need a break. You could hang out with me tomorrow." I immediately wonder if that isn't such a good idea. I just offered to spend possibly an entire day with a guy I barely know.

Before I can change my mind, Ben says, "All right."

"All right," I repeat, a little overwhelmed by what I've just set in motion. "How about I meet you at the coffee shop at eight?"

"Sure," he says.

"I'll see you then," I say, feeling awkward for the first time this evening.

I leave Ben on the sidewalk and head toward my motel. When I am almost at my room door, I turn back, and I'm surprised to see Ben standing exactly where I left him.

"What are you waiting for?" I call out to him.

"I'm waiting until you're inside," he says.

I turn around and continue walking. As much as I want to tell him to stop standing there and looking at this sad excuse for a motel, I think Ben watching me get all the way into my room *is* probably a good idea. It's dark out, and this isn't a great neighborhood.

I push the key into the lock of my door, but when I try to turn it, it won't turn.

I jiggle it and try again.

A gruff male voice groans from inside the room and starts an expletive-filled rant.

Heart racing, I back away from the door.

"What's wrong?" Ben yells out.

I head toward him. He meets me halfway.

"There's a man in my room!" I whisper to him.

"Are you sure you had the right room?" Ben asks.

My stomach drops. I turn and run toward the motel office.

"Where are you going?" Ben calls after me.

"I forgot to pay for my room today," I say, breathing hard.

Ben catches up with me. "Don't they just charge your credit card?"

"I'm paying cash. I have to pay every morning."

I collide with the office door and shove it open. Ben follows me inside.

The man at the desk looks up with a vacant gaze—different from the other times that I've seen him. There is an open bottle of whiskey next to him.

"Can I help you?" he asks.

"Where's my stuff?" I shout.

"Calm down." He points to some black trash bags behind the counter. "It's all right here."

I take a breath, ever-so-slightly relieved. "So, I forget to pay for one day and you go into my room, take out my things, and change the lock?"

"Actually, it's *my* room. You were just renting it ... 'til you stopped paying," he says. "By the way, I deducted twenty-five dollars from your deposit to pay for changing the lock."

I am livid, but the mistake was mine, and so I am at his mercy. "What am I supposed to do now?"

"If you pay for the night, I can put you in another room," he offers with a pointy smile that chills my blood.

"I want my stuff first," I say. The truth is, I don't have enough money in the waterproof wallet hanging around my neck to pay him for the room. Since I had been planning to spend today swimming at the beach, I'd left most of my cash inside my luggage, along with my camera and phone.

The man drops my suitcase and the trash bags on my side of the counter. My hands begin to tremble when I don't find my camera and phone tucked in with my socks, where I left them. I dig around in the suitcase and finally find them in a completely different spot—zipped into a compartment where I never would have put them. It makes my stomach turn to think that this man pawed through my things, even if he didn't take anything.

Ben kneels down next to me. "You don't have to stay here," he says.

I stare at my violated belongings. "I can't really afford anyplace else."

Without a pause, Ben says, "You can stay with me."

It's a completely absurd idea, but part of me wants to grab my things and go with Ben. His place has to be better than this. But I don't know Ben well enough to go home with him. It's just too risky.

"I'm fine," I say without looking at him.

I find my cash exactly where I hid it. I remove eighty dollars and pay the man at the desk.

"Room Twenty-nine," he says. "Same key."

I dump the contents of the trash bags into my suitcase, except for the flip-flops—which I pinch together between two fingers, their certainly germ-laden soles touching.

"Good night!" the man calls out as Ben and I leave the office. It sounds more like a taunt than a pleasantry.

A sign near the rusted vending machine indicates that Room Twenty-nine is located at the back of the property, and so we turn down the dingy, isolated alleyway that leads there. My room is the second to last in the row. All of the porch lights nearby are either burned out, smashed, or missing. I'm glad Ben is with me.

I turn my key in the lock for Room Twenty-nine, and the door clicks open. The smell of urine mixed with beer permeates the stale air inside the room. When I flip the light switch, at least ten large shiny brown insects race across the floor and disappear under the bed.

"Were those cockroaches?" I ask Ben, swallowing my disgust.

"I think so," Ben says, sounding equally disgusted.

I step forward, resigning myself to the fact that I will sleep here tonight.

I'm about to set my suitcase on the battered table when Ben steps in front of me.

"Erin, you deserve better than this," he says, looking into my eyes. "I'll help you find somewhere else to stay."

I shake my head. "I told you, I can't afford anywhere else."

"Then stay with me."

I stare at the soiled carpet beneath my feet. "I'm not spending the night at your place."

"It's not *my* place. It's my mom's," he says. "You'll

be safe there, I promise."

I can't trust Ben's promise of safety. Safety can never be completely guaranteed. And, even if it could be, it doesn't make sense to trust the promise of a stranger …

But maybe I need to follow him anyway.

I hurl my flip-flops into the trash can and head out the door.

"Where are you going?" Ben calls after me.

I answer without stopping. "To get my money back."

* * *

The man who accepted my money just minutes ago now appears to be asleep in his chair behind the counter in the motel office. I slam my room key down in front of him, and the man opens his eyes instantly. I doubt he was actually sleeping.

"Checking out!" I shout.

He barely hides his smirk. "But you already paid for the night."

"That room is unacceptable," I say.

"What's wrong with it?" he asks, feigning concern.

"It smells like urine. And there are cockroaches in there."

He raises his thick eyebrows. "Little girl, at the rate you're paying, that room is a gift."

"Well, I'm not staying there, so give me my money back."

He sighs and grabs a rusty aerosol can. "I'll go spray it down for ya, make it smell nice."

"No, I've had enough. I want my money back."

His gaze hardens. "I need to inspect the room first. For all I know, you trashed it."

My hands ball into fists. "Are you *kidding* me?"

The man comes out from behind the counter, carrying with him the smell of cigarettes mixed with alcohol. He looks me up and down, and then he sneers. "I'm *dead* serious."

I feel the blood drain from my face.

The man heads to the door. "Let's go have a look."

I shake my head. "We'll wait here."

He stares at me for a full minute before he grumbles, "Wait outside."

He follows Ben and me out of the office and locks the door behind us.

As soon as the man disappears around the corner, Ben says, "We should go."

"But I need to get my money back," I say.

"How much does he have?" Ben asks.

"Two hundred forty dollars. Wait … no … he subtracted twenty-five dollars from the deposit to change the lock. Two hundred fifteen dollars."

"It isn't worth it," Ben says. "He might come back here with a knife or a gun."

Ben's right. This could be dangerous. I'm willing to put *myself* in danger, but it isn't right to put Ben in danger too.

"You should go," I say. "I'll see you at the coffee shop tomorrow."

He shakes his head. "I'm not going to leave you here."

Before I can respond, the man comes back around the corner. I don't see any weapons with him, but that doesn't mean he doesn't have any. He eyes me suspiciously as he reopens the office. Dismissing the warnings blaring in my brain, I follow him inside. Ben is right behind me.

"Are we done?" I ask the man, trying to sound impatient rather than scared.

"The room isn't as I left it—" he starts.

Anger swells inside me. I feel like I'm about to explode.

"That's enough!" Ben exclaims.

"Ben, I've got this," I say through clenched teeth. I

turn to the man and say in a low voice, "You like taking advantage of people, don't you? It makes you feel like a big man, doesn't it? Well, you're NOT going to take advantage of *me*." I smash my fist against the counter. A cup of pens and a display of brochures crash to the ground with a hollow sound. "PUT MY MONEY ON THE COUNTER, NOW!"

Ben moves closer to me. "Just give her money back and we'll go away."

"Don't worry, he will," I say, then I stare at the man, unblinking, and growl, "I SAID, 'NOW!'"

Without breaking eye contact, the man reaches into his pocket, pulls out a few bills, and lays them on the counter. I count the money. It's exactly two hundred fifteen dollars. I stuff the cash into my pocket.

"Psycho bitch," the man says under his breath.

"*What* did you say?" Ben asks, approaching the desk.

"Don't bother, Ben," I say. "He's not worth it."

I grab my suitcase, and Ben and I leave the office, careful not to turn our backs to the man until we have left him far behind.

Neither of us says anything more until we are a few blocks north of the motel, and Ben asks me, "Where are we headed?"

"Your mom's house." I made that choice back when I hurled my flip-flops into the trash. I should probably consider looking for another motel, but it's late, the streets are devoid of all but the most unpleasant-looking of people, and the cold night air is starting to pass right through the sweater I pulled from my suitcase.

"Okay," Ben says.

He leads me past the coffee shop where we met and the café where we stopped for dinner, and then back into the same neighborhood we spent hours wandering earlier today.

"I'm sorry I put you in danger back there," I say to Ben as we turn up one of the streets.

He offers a tired grin. "It'll make a great story."

I imagine the story as Ben would tell it, and I can't help smiling. "I bet that jerk will think twice before he messes with a 'little girl' again."

"I have to admit, I didn't think you had it in you." Ben glances into my eyes, and I feel a spark, like electricity.

"Me neither." I admit.

Ben's expression darkens. "Makes me wonder if you have a death wish."

My stomach flips uncomfortably. "You think I have a death wish?"

He nods. "Yeah."

"I needed my money back," I counter.

"Right," Ben says, as if there's still more to be said.

"You think it's reckless to come home with you?" I ask, unsure whether I want to hear the answer.

"Maybe," he says.

"Am I making a mistake?" I ask.

"I'll try not to hurt you, Erin," he responds quietly.

My skin chills. "What is that supposed to mean?"

"I mean …" Ben starts, seeming a bit flustered. "It seems like you've been hurt a lot."

I'd thought I had done a decent job of hiding the effects of my trauma from Ben, but apparently, I haven't. Maybe I'm not capable of hiding my brokenness. But if Ben thinks I'm traumatized and have a death wish, why hasn't he come up with an excuse to separate from me? Why would he want to spend time with a damaged stranger?

Ben stops at the end of a brick walkway that leads to an enormous, two-story, Spanish-style home surrounded by a perfectly maintained garden of cacti. I don't see any lights on in the house, the only illumination is from the single light on the front porch. Ben starts up the walkway and then turns around and gives me a smile, as if our unsettling conversation never happened. "Are you

69

coming?"

My feet stay planted. "Shouldn't you let your mom know first?"

"She's out of town."

My stomach tightens. "When you said we were going to your mom's house, I thought she'd be here."

"Well, she's not," he says. "Is that okay?"

"Yeah," I say.

Shoving aside my fear, I follow Ben to the side door of the house.

"There's a spare key in the squirrel statue," he says. "You can hold onto it while you're here."

I pick up the ceramic squirrel and remove a key from the compartment in the bottom.

"The lock sticks a little," Ben continues. "Go ahead and try it out."

I have to work the key a bit to get it into the lock, but then the door pops open. I step into the darkened kitchen, and a black-and-white cat, wearing a jingle-bell collar, darts into the room to greet us.

"That's Bolt," Ben says.

I lean down and pet the cat as he purrs affectionately.

"The guest room is this way," Ben continues, directing me out of the kitchen.

Bolt follows us down a hallway lined with photos of far-away places: the Eiffel Tower, the Taj Mahal, the Sydney Opera House, and a snow-capped mountain that I think is Mount Fuji. We pass a bedroom with dark-blue walls speckled with tiny white stars and a model of the solar system hanging from the ceiling. It reminds me a bit of Star's childhood bedroom.

When we were eight years old, Star's parents allowed me and her to paint her room with an outer space theme. We were so proud of how it turned out that we literally cried tears of joy. My father would never have allowed me to do such a thing at his house, and I knew better than to ask. My bedroom had plain pink walls from the time I was born until the time I moved out when I turned eighteen.

"Whose room is that?" I ask Ben, gesturing toward the outer-space-themed room.

He hunches his shoulders, as if embarrassed. "That's my room. My mom designed it for me back when I was a kid and wanted to be an astronaut, and I never had the heart to update the décor. I'm kind of glad I didn't, though. Now it makes me feel nostalgic."

"I think it's great," I say. "Astronomy is cool."

His eyes brighten. "If you want, I can take you to Griffith Observatory."

"Yeah, maybe," I say, unsure if I'll ever feel ready to go back there.

Ben leads me into an immaculate room decorated in pink and green floral prints. The light scent of peaches greets me—likely from the crystal bowl of potpourri on the nightstand.

"There are clean towels in the guest bathroom," Ben says, pointing toward a slightly open door. "Do you need anything else?"

"No," I say. "Thank you."

He stands there, looking at me, his expression unreadable. I'm not sure what he's waiting for, but he doesn't wait long. "Good night then."

"Good night."

Ben exits the room, followed by Bolt, and I shut the door behind them. There is no lock. I consider for a moment wedging the nightstand and desk against the door to form a makeshift barricade, like I did at the motel, but that won't stop Ben from doing me harm if that is his intention. And so instead, I lodge a mouse-shaped cat toy under the door. It won't deter anyone from entering the room, but at least I'll know if someone opens the door, even a little, while I'm asleep.

I close my eyes and take a deep breath of the peach-scented air. It feels safe here, but I know there is nowhere in the world that is truly safe. Harm can come when you least expect it. Safety is just an illusion that we allow ourselves to believe so we can rest.

And now, whether I am safe or not, I desperately need to rest.

Chapter Eight

Rough hands grab hold of me. They pin my arms against my sides, and my assailant pulls my body against his. I want to scream, but I can't …

Because I am underwater.

I am pulled through a shattered window, and the broken glass scrapes my shins, probably drawing blood. My lungs are pleading for oxygen. That soon becomes the only thing I can think about. I have to force myself not to inhale, but my resolve is weakening. I feel myself fading. I can't let myself fade. If I do, I'll breathe. If I breathe, I'll drown. And I don't want to drown.

Suddenly, air splashes against my face. I suck it in between desperate hacking coughs. My lungs feel as if they're on fire. Every breath burns, and coughing is sheer agony, but I need to breathe, and I can't make myself stop coughing.

Hands pull me up onto a slab of concrete that juts out into the water. My body instinctively curls into the fetal position, but I fight it. I need to find Dylan, Star, and Mateo.

I scan the shoreline, and I spot someone else being pulled from the water. *It's Star!*

"Star!" I crawl to her, the bottom of my dress tearing on the sharp rocks.

When Star sees my face, relief washes over her. "Erin!" she croaks out between coughs.

A man wraps a sweatshirt over my bare shoulders. Dylan's jacket isn't there anymore. I don't remember losing it, but it's gone.

Another man offers a sweatshirt to Star.

"Where are … the other people … who were in the limo?" I ask him, breathless.

"We've got them over there," he says, pointing to a rocky area a few feet away.

Star and I stagger to our feet and rush over to where he pointed.

When we get there, Star drops to her knees beside Mateo. His head is wrapped in a blood-soaked t-shirt. Our driver is lying on the rocks nearby, breathing hard. I don't see Dylan anywhere.

"Where's Dylan?" I ask Mateo urgently.

"I … don't know." He tries to stand but topples over.

Star looks at him with concern. "You should lie down."

I grab the arm of a man nearby. "Where's Dylan?"

"There's someone over there," he says, pointing at our driver.

I shake my head. "That's not him. There's still one more person in the limo."

"We've got guys in the water, searching," he tries to reassure me.

"Dylan!" I shout, crawling back toward the water.

The man grabs my arm, preventing me from jumping in. "You need to stay here."

"My boyfriend is *underwater*!" I yell, trying to free myself from his grip. "He was unconscious. I need to find him."

"You're in no condition to go back out there," the man says.

He's right. But I don't care. I can't wait here and do nothing. Unfortunately, I don't have a choice. The man isn't releasing me from his vice-like grip.

And then his hold on me suddenly loosens. "Is that your friend?" he asks me.

He moves out of the way just enough that I can see two people in the water towing Dylan toward us at breakneck speed. I help pull him onto the jagged concrete. His body is limp. He's not responding to anything. And it doesn't look like he's breathing.

I shout his name over and over, but he doesn't seem to hear me.

Star starts doing CPR on Dylan, and horror fills my chest.

Dylan can't need CPR.

I take Dylan's hand. The hand that once held tightly onto mine, our fingers intertwined. The hand that caressed my face as if I was the most precious person he'd ever known. The hand that, just minutes ago, gently stroked the hair away from my eyes before he leaned in to kiss me.

His hand is so cold. I take the sweatshirt from my shoulders and wrap it around Dylan's hand. Trying to keep this one part of him warm.

Dylan is going to wake up, I tell myself. *He is going to be okay.*

But deep down, somewhere in my gut, I know that he is *not* going to be okay.

Nothing is ever going to be okay again.

My eyelids snap open.

I sit up, feeling nauseous, breathing hard and fast. Through blurry eyes, I take in the pretty florals of Ben's guest room. Everything is neat and clean and safe-looking. But nothing, not even this perfect room, could protect me from my nightmares.

I swallow down the acid that's burning my throat and force myself out of bed. In the bathroom, I splash my face with cold water. I can't let Ben see me like this. Last night, he said he knows that I've been hurt, but I don't want him to see how truly broken I am.

I wait until my face looks presentable before I tentatively open the guest room door. Bolt comes running to greet me, the bell on his collar jingling. I take a moment to pet him, and then I follow the sound of a TV to the kitchen. My heart speeds when I see Ben sitting at the kitchen table, sipping a cup of tea.

"Good morning," he says as if it's the most normal thing in the world to have a virtual stranger walk into his mom's kitchen first thing in the morning. Then again, considering how easily he invited me here, maybe for Ben it is.

I take a breath, searching for strength. "Good morning," I answer.

"Help yourself to whatever's in the cabinet and the fridge," Ben offers.

After a brief forage, I grab a jar of almond butter and a bag of granola, along with a glass of water, a bowl, and a spoon, and I join Ben at the table. On the TV, a meteorologist is reviewing the forecast. His graphic shows seven days of bright-yellow suns.

I spoon some almond butter onto the granola and dig in.

"So, what's on tap for today?" Ben asks me.

I think I need to take a break from memories. I want to do something that my friends and I had planned to do but didn't get around to.

"I'm thinking about going to see the stars in the sidewalk along Hollywood Boulevard and the celebrity hand and footprints …" I start, but then my attention is captured by a photo that just appeared on the TV screen. A picture of a carefree girl wearing a swimsuit patterned with smiley-faced flowers. "That's the girl from the ocean," I breathe.

The reporter continues, "The girl's body was discovered by a swimmer yesterday morning, off the beach in Santa Monica."

"The swimmer was you?" Ben asks.

I nod.

The reporter goes on, "Funeral services will be held for Alexis Reynolds at Saint Charles Borromeo Church tomorrow afternoon at five. Members of the public are invited to attend."

"You should go to the funeral," Ben says.

I push my almond-butter-coated spoon into the granola, no longer hungry. "I didn't know her."

"You kind of met."

I shake my head. "I hate funerals. I didn't even go to my best friends' funerals."

Ben's eyes narrow. "Your best friends died?"

"Yeah," I say. "They're all dead."

"How'd they die?" he asks.

I take a sip of water, fighting the urge to cry. "I don't want to talk about that, okay?"

"Okay," Ben says, and then he adds, "But I still think you should go to Alexis's funeral."

"I'll think about it," I say. And I will.

But I've already decided that I won't go.

* * *

A man in a tattered superhero costume wanders past Ben and me as we walk along a sidewalk adorned with brass-and-stone stars sporting the names of celebrities. Ahead of us, a disheveled woman in grimy clothes leans against a wall, clutching a crumpled dollar bill in her hand, and talking loudly with someone who isn't there.

I turn to Ben. "This place makes me sad." It's the same sense of despair that I've felt in other cities, and in other parts of Los Angeles, but here on Hollywood Boulevard, with reminders of so many dreams come true stuck into the sidewalk, it's even more disheartening.

"Maybe you'll like the celebrity hand and footprints better," Ben offers.

He leads me into a courtyard where tourists mill around snapping photos of the ground. I half-heartedly look down at the hand and shoeprints and the autographs preserved in cement.

"Hey!" Ben calls out "My feet are the same size as Indiana Jones'!"

He's standing in Harrison Ford's footprints, smiling so broadly that he looks goofy. His unbridled enthusiasm makes me smile too.

"Wait a second. I want to get a photo of you," I say, pulling out my camera.

Ben puts on an even bigger grin, and I snap a picture. It's the first photo I've taken since I arrived in Los Angeles. I tuck my camera into my pocket and look for footprints to fit my sneakers into. Most of the women were wearing heels when their footprints were preserved, so it's hard to tell if our feet are the same size. I finally find an exact match.

"My feet are the same size as Meryl Streep's," I shout out to Ben.

He jogs over. "Let's get a picture."

I hold out my camera to a fellow tourist and ask him, "Would you mind taking a picture of us?"

Ben moves closer to me and, suddenly, I feel a palpable energy rise between us, along with feelings that I hadn't expected to feel. My heart races. I take a shaky breath, trying to calm myself down, as the man aims my camera.

"*Ichi, ni, san*," he says, and then he snaps a photo and hands the camera back to me.

"*Domo arigato gozaimasu*," Ben says to him.

I nod my head in agreement, assuming, based on the man's polite bow, that Ben said something nice.

"What did you say to him?" I ask Ben as we walk away.

"'Thank you very much' in Japanese," he answers.

"You speak Japanese?"

"My mom taught me a bunch of languages when I was a kid. She told me that learning different languages is like traveling the world without leaving home."

"Does she travel a lot?"

"No," Ben says. "The trip she's on now is the first one she's taken in a long time."

"Where did she go?" I ask.

"Paris," he replies, and then he says, "Come on. There's something I want to show you."

"What?" I ask, nervously.

"It's a surprise," he says.

"I don't like surprises." I used to like them, but I don't anymore.

Ben offers his hand. "Do you trust me?"

I stare at his hand, but I don't accept it. "I want to …"

"Good enough." He turns and starts walking away.

I tuck my camera into my pocket, and I follow him back along the sidewalk of Hollywood Boulevard. He stops in front of an ordinary-looking movie theater box office.

"You want to see a movie?" I ask, puzzled.

"Sort of." He takes out his wallet and checks the movie listings. "Let's go see … *The Darkness Outside*."

"Okay, but it's on me." Taking Ben to a movie is the least I can do to thank him for letting me stay with him last night. I slide some cash to the lady on the other side of the glass. "Two adults for *The Darkness Outside*," I tell her.

She hands me the tickets and my change. I stuff the money into my wallet and follow Ben toward a theatre that looms at the far end of the courtyard where we saw the hand and footprints. As I pass Ben his ticket, his fingers brush lightly against mine, and I feel a tingling that makes my stomach churn. I jerk my hand back, and the ticket slips and lands in a footprint.

I look away as Ben scoops the ticket off the ground. "Sorry," I mumble.

"It's okay," Ben says gently.

Our gaze meets, but his expression is unreadable

Did Ben feel the tingling too? Was he upset that I pulled away?

Without saying anything, he turns and starts toward one of the three golden doors flanked by tall columns encircled by menacing spiked metal masks.

I catch up with him and ask, "So what's this movie about?"

Ben shrugs. "I have no idea."

"Then why do you want to see it?" I ask as I step into the theater entryway.

And then I gasp. Aside from the modern concession stand straight ahead of us, we could be in the reception area of an elegant hotel half a world away. The dark walls are adorned with elaborate painted images of ancient China. An intricate, lantern-like chandelier hangs above us. The crimson carpet features the image of a dragon.

"They use this theater for movie premieres," Ben says. "But when they're not having a premiere, anyone can see a movie here."

We descend into an atmospheric auditorium that is an even grander version of the lobby. Reds, browns, and golds cover the fantastic walls. There must be at least a hundred people occupying the seats, but the massive theater feels nearly empty. As I sink into a plush velvet seat, the scarlet curtain decorated with golden palm trees begins to part, revealing a tremendous movie screen.

Ben plops down in the seat next to me. "Do you like it?" he whispers.

I smile. "I love it."

* * *

"That movie was amazing!" I gush as Ben and I exit the theater. "I kept thinking I knew what was going to happen next, but I was completely wrong."

"What movie did you see?" a woman, who had been admiring the footprints in the theater courtyard, asks me.

"*The Darkness Outside*," I tell her. "I'd definitely recommend seeing it here. The theater is absolutely gorgeous."

"My daughter and I have been wanting to see that

movie ever since we finished the book," the woman says, and then she turns to a teenage girl beside her. "Do you want to see *The Darkness Outside* tomorrow after our Hollywood Sign hike?"

"Oh, yes!" the girl says.

"You can hike to the Hollywood Sign?" I ask the woman.

"There's a trail that takes you just above it," she answers.

"I could use a hike," Ben says.

"I'll show you how to get there." The woman takes out her phone, pulls up a map, and points out the trailhead. It isn't too far from a stop of the Metro train that Ben and I took to get here.

Before she puts her phone away, she asks, "Would you mind taking a photo of my daughter and me with the theater?"

I accept her phone. "No problem."

The woman and the girl pose beside one of the fanciful stone creatures at the theater entrance. Together, they mug for the camera, the way Dylan, Star, Mateo, and I used to. I swallow against the lump in my throat and snap a picture.

"Do you want me to take a photo for you?" the woman offers.

"Sure." I trade my camera for her phone and wave Ben over.

I feel that disconcerting tingling again when he leans close to me for the photo.

"Smile!" the woman calls out to us as she aims the camera.

I smile, but I can't shake my unease. Just days ago, Ben was a random stranger in a coffee shop. But now my relationship with him feels like it's hurtling toward something more than a friendship. Something that feels … inevitable.

And that scares me to death.

* * *

"You seem sad," Ben says, as we walk past one of the little bungalows that fit, like pieces of a giant jigsaw puzzle, onto the base of the mountain that sports the Hollywood Sign.

"Why do you think that?" I ask.

"I see it in your eyes," he says.

"How can you see that in my eyes?" I ask, a little more defensively than I meant to.

"I guess because I know what it's like to feel that way," he says.

"You do?"

Ben looks at the ground, and his hair falls toward his face, the way it does when he types on his laptop. "Can I tell you a story?"

So far, I've loved Ben's stories, but I get the feeling I won't like this one.

I take a deep breath. "Okay."

We walk for a while before he speaks again, "When I was a kid, my father tended to use me as a punching bag. He left my face, arms, and legs alone, so people wouldn't see the bruises." Ben's voice is steady and unaffected, as if he's talking about the weather rather than the beating of a child.

He continues, "I thought I would finally escape from my father when I went off to college, but when it came time to apply, he insisted on choosing the school. He said that I would have to live at home and commute to campus. He did the same thing for law school. And then, when it came time to start thinking about my future, he had that all figured out too. My father was well-respected in the community. He had a lot of money, and a lot of power. I began to realize that he was going to find some way to control me for the rest of his life."

Ben pauses for a deep breath. I take one too and hold it as he continues, "My father had a samurai sword that he was exceptionally proud of—he bought it during a trip to Japan. He had it hung on the wall of his office in downtown LA. One morning, I woke up early, rode the Metro to his office, and took the sword off the wall. Then I stabbed myself in the chest."

My heart burns with pain as Ben goes on, "I woke up in a hospital. I had tubes coming out of places that should never have tubes in them. Even with all of the painkillers flowing into my IV, it was the worst physical pain I'd ever experienced.

"A social worker came to talk to me. She asked about all of the old scars on my body, the ones from my father's beatings. I told her they were from accidents. Then she brought in an oncologist, and they told me I had cancer. The ER doctors had discovered it when they did the blood tests they do on trauma patients. While everyone was talking, all I kept thinking was that I wished I had died on the floor of my father's office."

Before I can respond, Ben starts speaking again, "I didn't think my life would ever get any better. But it *did* get better. I got transferred to the oncology unit and started chemo which, as bad as it was, wasn't nearly as bad as living with my father. My oncologist set me up with a therapist. One day, I told her the truth about my past. That same night, my father got in his favorite car, and he drove off. After a couple of months of not hearing from him, I began to experience something that I hadn't felt in years ... hope."

I open my mouth, wishing I could figure out something appropriate to say in response, but I can't think of any words that begin to express the deep ache in my heart where I feel the pain of Ben's wounds meet the pain of mine.

We walk in silence until Ben breaks it by pointing to a nearby sign and reading it with surprising enthusiasm, "Horseback tours in the Hollywood Hills!"

There's a big red arrow on the sign pointing up the dirt road ahead.

"You want to go for a horseback ride?" Ben asks me.

I have absolutely no desire to go on a horseback ride, but he sounds so thrilled with the idea that I say, "Sure."

Ben takes off running, and I race after him. We sprint up the dusty road until we arrive at a large horse enclosure. Ben stops short, and I nearly collide with him.

The horses are much larger than I thought they would be. I guess I was picturing the ponies I've seen toddlers riding at fairs.

"Have you ridden a horse before?" Ben asks me as he admires the horses.

I swallow. "I don't think so. Have you?"

"I used to ride all the time. But I haven't been on a horse since I was eight."

"Why not?" I ask.

"I'll tell you after."

He continues slowly up the road.

I take a deep breath and follow him.

Chapter Nine

I am definitely not enjoying my horseback ride, mostly because my assigned horse insists on walking on the very outermost edge of the dirt trail, where one misstep would send us on a plunge down a steep mountainside that is covered in prickly shrubs.

Ahead of me—also on horseback—are three tourists from Australia, our guide, and Ben. We all wear yellow plastic helmets, except for our guide, who wears a cowboy hat. But, even in his dorky helmet, Ben looks attractive.

My horse picks up her pace, moving ahead of Ben's, as if she's in some kind of unofficial race. I'm not sure whether it would annoy her if I try slowing her down, so I don't. I don't want to do anything that might perturb the animal that is largely responsible for whether or not I finish this experience in one piece.

Now I can't see Ben unless I turn around, something I'm too anxious to try. But I really wish I could see him. Seeing Ben in front of me was exactly what I needed to keep myself from freaking out. Now, panic rises unfettered in my chest.

"You don't look like you're having fun," Ben calls out from behind me.

"I'm too nervous to have fun," I mutter at him.

Ben increases the speed of his horse to match mine. "Want some advice?"

"Sure," I say.

"When it comes to horses like these, if you let them, they'll take you exactly where you need to go," he says. "You just have to trust the horse."

Before I can respond, my horse increases her pace yet again, moving far ahead of Ben's. I wonder if she is sensing my fear, trying to escape it.

I close my eyes and take a deep breath, willing myself to calm down, counting in my head. *One Mississippi, Two Mississippi, Three Mississippi. Three Mississippi, Two Mississippi, One Mississippi.*

I feel myself shift a little, and my heart speeds. I open my eyes and force myself to take another slow breath, trying to follow Ben's advice, trying to trust my horse.

And then, something changes. For the first time, the horse and I begin to move *together*. Like we are one animal. It feels … like magic.

I begin to notice everything around me, as the world has suddenly come into sharp focus. Skinny tree branches sway in the breeze. The cowboy hat on our guide bobs gently up and down. Glimmers of light reflect off the Pacific Ocean. It is all so … beautiful.

Hoofbeats approach me, almost matching the rhythm of my heart. Ben and his horse appear by my side once more. Ben doesn't say anything and neither do I. But I feel that palpable energy between us again. It seems to be growing more intense by the second.

And when my gaze meets his, I am certain that Ben feels it too.

* * *

Ben and I—and our horses—are the last ones to join our group at the top of Mount Hollywood. The view here has to be one of the most spectacular in all of Los Angeles: three hundred sixty degrees of hills, mountains, and sprawling cities.

My horse parks herself next to Ben's, facing Mount Lee, where the Hollywood Sign resides. Ben gives me a smile that reveals a dimple in his right cheek, then he turns his gaze to the Hollywood Sign, our next destination.

I try to imagine what it might be like to stand there with Ben, right above the Hollywood Sign letters, as the wind whips through our hair. Strangely, I picture him wrapping his arms around me and drawing me close to him. I imagine him looking deep into my eyes, as if he wants to kiss me. And then my eyes flutter closed, and I feel the warmth of his lips against mine. Even the thought of kissing Ben should make me feel anxious. But, inexplicably, I feel—

"Ready?" Ben asks.

I shake off my daydream and snap back into the present: Ben and me on horseback at the top of Mount Hollywood. Our bodies not touching at all.

Our guide is starting to lead our group back down the mountain.

Ben's horse turns to go. And my horse follows.

* * *

It has been almost an hour since Ben and I dropped off our horses at the ranch and began our hike up the trails that wind their way to the Hollywood Sign. We've spent most of our hike in silence but, now, with my muscles beginning to ache, I feel like conversation might be a good distraction.

"You seemed incredibly comfortable on that horse," I say to Ben.

"I used to ride competitively," he says, keeping his focus on the trail. "Riding was my life."

"So what happened?" I ask.

"It's kind of a long story."

"If you're willing to tell it, I want to hear it."

Ben glances toward me. "Even after that last one?"

I nod. "Especially after that last one."

Ben pauses beside a wooden fence that separates us from the steep mountainside. He looks toward the purple mountains that rise up beyond a city whose name I don't know, and he inhales. "I had this horse: Marge. She was a great horse. The best. On the day of one of my big competitions, I noticed that Marge seemed strangely sensitive. Every little noise bothered her. My father said she must be having a bad day, but she'd never had bad days before. Because of the competition, I had to ride her anyway. At the beginning, she was doing all right. But then she missed a jump. On the next one, she jumped way too high. When she landed, she lost her footing, and we fell. I hit my head and went unconscious. Fortunately, when I woke up, aside from a bad headache, I was fine. I asked about Marge, and my father said she was gone. He'd *sold* her. I was furious. I loved that horse.

"A few months later, I overheard my father telling my mom that it was *her* fault Marge had been spooked that day. Apparently, my mom had forgotten to do something or other for my father and, in front of Marge, they'd had an 'argument'—which was the word that my father used for his one-sided beratings of my mom. I remember that, just before I took Marge out to the arena, when my father came in to wish me good luck, Marge had gotten very upset. I couldn't calm her down. Now I know why. But, even once I found out the truth, there was nothing I could do to get her back."

Ben turns and starts walking again. I stay right beside him as the trail wraps around the mountain. And then I follow him to a tall chain-link fence. Ben grips onto it with both hands and peers through it. When I gaze through the fence, I see the corrugated backsides of the famous Hollywood Sign letters just below us. Beyond them are stunning mansion-covered hills. Not far away, there's a glistening blue-green lake nestled in a valley of extravagant homes.

Ben and I stand there for a while, taking in the view, and then he turns toward me. "Thank you for inviting me to hang out with you today. I feel like, tomorrow, I might actually be able to start writing something."

"That's wonderful," I say, but my stomach sinks. I'd been planning to invite Ben to join me again tomorrow, but I guess that isn't going to happen. Of course, I'm glad he feels ready to write, but I was hoping to spend another day with him. I feel empty at the thought of spending tomorrow without Ben.

"We should probably head back," he says.

"Right," I say.

As we hike back down Mount Lee, I will time to slow down.

But I feel like it only moves faster.

* * *

At a picnic table under the willow tree in his backyard, Ben and I relive the highlights of our day while sharing take-out Thai food. Once the sun starts to leave the sky and the air begins to chill, we collect what remains of our dinner and head back toward the house, along a meandering stone path lined with sweet-smelling flowers.

As we pass the sparkling pool and hot tub, Ben asks, "Want to take a dip in the hot tub?"

The idea of soothing my sore muscles in the warm water is inviting. At the same time, the thought of sitting in a hot tub with Ben makes my stomach twist with unease.

But I hear myself say, "Okay."

We separate to go put on our swimsuits. After I put mine on, I pull my shorts and t-shirt on over it and grab a towel. By the time I make it back to the hot tub, Ben is already in the water.

Ben regards my shorts and t-shirt. "Did you change your mind?"

"No," I say.

I'm not sure why I put my clothes on over my swimsuit for the quick walk to the hot tub. I could have just wrapped the towel around me.

Ben averts his eyes as I remove my shirt and shorts and step into the tub. It is only after I am fully enveloped in the water that he returns his gaze to me. When he does, he shifts his position, and I catch a glimpse of a scar on his shoulder. I see a flash of shame in Ben's eyes.

"I have scars too," I admit. "Deep inside me."

He nods. "I know."

I wonder if Ben sensed that about me from the moment we met. Maybe I sensed that about him as well. Maybe that's why we bonded so quickly.

Ben pulls himself out of the hot tub and sits on the edge, allowing me to see him more fully. He's wearing tight navy-blue swim trunks, and his chest is rippled with perfect muscles. He looks like a swimsuit model ... aside from the scars. So many of them. Violating his beautiful body. What I see hurts me down to my very core.

Suddenly, I feel like there's something I need to do. But not just for me. Maybe for both of us.

"May I hug you?" I ask Ben.

His shoulders tense. "Now?"

"Is that okay?"

He inhales uncomfortably. "I don't know if that's a good idea, Erin."

"I don't know either." I look into his eyes. "But I still want to."

Ben holds my gaze for a long time, then he exhales. "Okay."

I swim across the hot tub and then stand on the seat in front of Ben, our bodies just inches apart. My heart races. My breaths quicken. My head tells me to stop, but my heart tells me to go on.

I close my eyes and wrap my arms around Ben as tightly as I can. And he wraps his arms around me, just as tightly. Our hearts pound furiously. Our chests rise and fall. Heat radiates from Ben's skin to mine.

I stay there, in Ben's arms. Until we both stop trembling.

Chapter Ten

When I awaken, the first thing I notice is the muffled clicking of a keyboard. I inhale the scent of peach potpourri, climb out of bed, and make my way to the door of Ben's guest room. As I open it, I accidentally kick the cat toy that I once used as an intruder detector all the way into the living room. Last night, I didn't wedge it under the door before I went to bed. That's probably because, when Ben held me in his arms in the hot tub, I felt so safe that I can't imagine he would ever attempt to harm me.

I walk quietly to Ben's bedroom doorway and watch him type on his laptop. He's wearing blue checked boxers, brown socks, and a faded gray t-shirt, probably the clothes he slept in.

He looks up at me.

"Are you *writing*?" I ask him.

"Yes," he says.

I try to read his expression, but I can't. "For real?"

He smiles, relief washing over his face. "Yes."

I run over to him. "Can I see?"

Ben takes me by the waist and spins me away from the screen. "Not yet."

Even though I am no longer attempting to look at his laptop, Ben's hands remain on my hips, some of his fingers resting on the bare skin around my waist. As I stare into his eyes, I get the feeling that he might want to kiss me. And I think I want to kiss him too. We didn't kiss last night. It didn't seem right then. But now, things feel different …

Suddenly, Ben removes his hands from my waist, as if he was unsettled to discover they were there.

I break the awkward silence that follows, "I guess I'll go to the kitchen and have breakfast."

Ben nods. "I'm almost done writing this scene. I'll meet you there in a few minutes."

When I enter the living room, Bolt is lying on the floor, attempting to disembowel his toy mouse with his back claws. He discards the toy and runs to me, purring loudly. I pet him for a minute, and then we both head to the kitchen. Bolt crunches on cat kibble as I grab the almond butter and granola from the cabinet, half-watching the news.

I'm pouring granola over a mound of almond butter when Ben enters the kitchen, fills a glass of water, and sits down across from me. "What are your plans for today?" he asks.

"I thought I'd check out the Los Angeles Zoo." That's something else that my friends and I talked about doing but didn't get around to.

"How are you going to get there?" he asks.

"The bus," I say, taking a bite of granola.

"If you can drive a stick-shift, you can borrow the car." Ben points to the kitchen door. "The keys are on the hook."

I force the granola down my throat. "You're offering to let me borrow *your car*?" I ask, incredulous.

He shrugs. "It's my father's car."

Okay, but still ... "What if I drive off and never come back?"

He shakes his head. "You won't."

He's right, of course.

I cock my head. "You don't know me well enough to say that."

"Yes, I do," he says, and then he adds, "Besides, if you stole that car, no one would miss it."

He grabs a breakfast bar from the cabinet and heads back down the hallway.

And then I hear him shut his bedroom door.

* * *

After I finish my breakfast, I throw on a pair of shorts and a t-shirt, and I take the car key from the hook by the door. I feel a little hesitant to borrow a car, but driving will certainly be more pleasant than taking the circuitous bus trip I had planned.

Before I head out, I go to Ben's bedroom to let him know I'm leaving. His door is open now, but I don't see him inside the room. I knock on the doorjamb. "Ben?"

"One second," he calls out from a room attached to his. A second or so later, he comes around the corner, easing a t-shirt over his glistening, freshly washed hair.

"I wanted to wish you a good day writing," I say, catching a glimpse of his chest. It still hurts me to see his scars.

"Would you mind if I join you today?" Ben asks.

I smile knowingly. "You had second thoughts about me driving off with the car, didn't you?"

"No. I've been writing since three in the morning. I think I'm done for now," he says. "So what do you think? Do you want company?"

I nod. "Absolutely."

Ben stuffs his wallet into his pocket and follows me to the garage. When I open the door, I do a double take. Morning sunlight sparkles off the hood of a sleek black sports car. I don't know much about cars, but this one looks extremely expensive. I try to pass the keychain to Ben, but he pushes it away.

"Aren't you going to drive?" I ask.

"My license was suspended," Ben says.

I turn toward him, wondering if he's joking, but his expression tells me that he isn't.

"Why was your license suspended?" I ask hesitantly.

"My father's license was revoked because he had a bunch of DUIs," he starts. "About a year ago, he dragged me out to his favorite restaurant to celebrate a big case he'd won. I had a couple of drinks, because my father insisted I drink 'for him.' He couldn't have any alcohol that night, because he was on antibiotics for a skin infection, so he drove us home. On the way, he took a curve too fast and hit a car. Fortunately, no one was hurt. He told the police I was the one who'd been driving. I didn't bother arguing. Arguing with my father never got me anywhere. My license was suspended for a year because it was my 'second offense.'"

"Your *second* offense?" I ask.

"It wasn't the first time my father did that to me," Ben says. "He was a pretty bad driver."

I look into his eyes. "You deserved so much better than him."

"Most people don't get the life they deserve," Ben says.

I unlock the car doors and slide into the driver's seat. Ben slips into the passenger's seat. Then I push the ignition button, and the engine comes alive.

"You can retract the roof if you want," Ben says, pointing to a button on the dash.

I press it and, almost soundlessly, the car's roof folds back and hides itself in the trunk.

"This car is awesome!" I say. And then I remember whose car this is. "Sorry, I—"

"It's okay," Ben says. "The car *is* awesome."

"I'm surprised your father didn't take it with him."

Ben shrugs awkwardly. "He drove off in his other one, and never came back." From Ben's tone, I can sense the hurt he's trying to hide. But before I can say anything in response, he fastens his seatbelt and says, "Let's go."

I put on my seatbelt, take a deep breath, and shift the car into first gear.

* * *

In a landscaped area with boulders, trees, logs, and a stream, a Sumatran tiger strides along a dirt path. All of a sudden, a tiny tiger cub leaps out from behind a log and pounces on the adult's hindquarters. A second cub jumps out from behind a bush and launches an attack on the first one, rolling onto his back and swatting at the first cub with his paws. The crowd of zoo-goers around us murmurs with delight.

A youngish man arrives holding a little girl in his arms. Ben and I scoot over, so they can slip in beside us along the fence of the tigers' enclosure.

"Kitties!" the girl exclaims as she catches her first glimpse of the tigers.

"They're not *kitties*. Those are *tigers*," the man corrects her coldly.

"Kitties!" the girl says once more. The child—who can't be more than three years old—probably can't tell the difference.

The man shakes his head. "They're *tigers*. And you're a ditz just like your mommy."

He places the girl on the ground, where she can no longer see the tigers. She strains to peer over the enclosure's fence, but she's much too small to see over the top.

Tears of frustration fill the little girl's eyes as she

holds her arms out to the man, begging him to pick her up again. "Kitties! Kitties!" she pleads, but the man ignores her.

Ben's right hand forms a fist as he glares at the man. Nervous about what might transpire, I lead Ben away.

As soon as we're out of earshot of the man, I ask, "Were you going to punch that guy?"

"No," Ben says, as if he's disappointed in himself.

"Did he remind you of your father?" I ask.

Ben's gaze falls to the ground. "Yeah."

"He reminded me of my father too," I say.

Ben turns toward me. "That's the first time you've said anything about your family."

"I don't like talking about my family."

Ben looks back at the ground. "Me neither."

But Ben has already shared so much about his family with me.

"I'm glad you did," I say softly.

"I wish *you* would," he says even softer.

I don't ask why. I'm pretty sure I know the answer. I think Ben wants to know me the same way I want to know him. I think he wants to hear about more than just the superficial stuff that people might share in polite conversation. I think he wants to see the *real* me.

I take a breath. "When I was a kid, every morning,

even on Saturdays and Sundays, my father would get up, go to work, come home, play games on his computer, and then go to bed. He never wanted to have anything to do with me. Whenever we spent time together, it was painfully obvious that he couldn't wait for our time together to be over. I tried so hard to make him proud. I didn't get into trouble. I did really well in school, but when I gave him my report cards to sign, he barely even looked at them. I taught myself chess, because it was my father's favorite game, but he never wanted to play with me. As soon as I turned eighteen, I moved out of his house and never went back.

"On the night of my twenty-fifth birthday, my best friends rented a limo, and we rode around our hometown, visiting all of our favorite spots. At the end of the night, our limo driver wasn't answering our texts. It was late, everything was closed, and we were freezing cold. My father's house was a ten-minute walk away, so I called him to ask if we could hang out there until we could get in touch with our driver or find another way home.

"As soon as he heard my voice, he sounded annoyed. Before I could tell him what was going on, he said that it was too late to be calling him unless it was a life-threatening emergency. He asked if I had a life-threatening emergency. I said, 'No.' That's when the limo driver finally responded to our texts." I swallow. "On our way home, a truck drifted into our lane. Our driver swerved to avoid it, but we crashed through a barricade and landed in a pond. Dylan was dead by the time we got him out of the water. Mateo died on the way to the hospital. If it hadn't been for a bus full of college guys coming back from a wedding, my friend Star and I would have died that night too. It was a miracle that they saw our limo go into the water. But even that miracle wasn't enough to save Dylan and Mateo."

I steady my voice and continue, "Even if my father had agreed to let us come over, it wouldn't have made a difference. When our driver responded to our texts, I would have called him right back and told him that we got a ride. But still ..."

Ben nods. "I understand."

I think Ben is the only person I've ever met who I actually *does* understand. Star, Dylan, and Mateo knew about my relationship with my father, and they were extremely supportive, but they didn't *understand*. They all had great dads. Dylan, Star, Mateo, and their families were the closest thing to a family that I had, until the accident took everything away.

Ben and I continue down a path to a giant makeshift jungle gym surrounded by netting, where reddish-brown orangutans deftly scale a network of ropes. On the ground, a tiny orangutan baby is cradled in the arms of an adult—probably his mother.

The baby reaches toward a nearby rope, but his fingertips barely graze it. The mother orangutan gives him what looks like a hug and then loosens her embrace enough that, when the baby reaches again, his tiny fingers are able to wrap around the rope. He pulls himself toward it, almost wriggling out of his mother's arms, but then seems to reconsider. He lets go of the rope, grabs hold of his mother, and snuggles against her chest.

"What about your mom?" Ben asks me.

I stare at the orangutan cuddling her baby. "She left me when I was four years old."

* * *

A hoofed animal balances on impossibly delicate hind legs and nibbles at some leaves on a tree. According to the sign posted outside the enclosure, she's a gerenuk. Another gerenuk stands nearby, chewing. When she swallows, a small bulge appears at the top of her long, skinny neck and travels down, disappearing into her body. A moment later, the bulge reappears at the bottom of her neck and travels back up. Then she starts chewing again.

"You can *see* them regurgitate!" I exclaim.

Ben laughs.

My cheeks flush. "I guess that's kind of gross."

Ben smiles enough that his dimple shows. "Speaking of regurgitation, are you hungry?"

I laugh. "A little."

I look at my watch. *It's almost four-thirty.* I wonder where the day went.

"We could go to dinner at CityWalk," Ben suggests.

CityWalk is an open-air shopping mall that looks as if it was ripped out of a cartoon world and dropped into reality. During my last trip to L.A., my friends and I spent an evening there after our day at Universal Studios Hollywood theme park. We ate at Saddle Ranch Chop House, where Star rode the mechanical bull in the dining room for a full minute while everyone cheered her on. Then we wandered in and out of the shops and shared a deliciously gooey cinnamon bun for dessert.

I had been planning to go to CityWalk on this trip too, but after my recent experiences at the observatory and the beach, I've been thinking that I'd rather go somewhere else—*anywhere else*—than a place I visited with my friends. I don't feel strong enough to face any more memories, but maybe I need to try. And maybe it would be easier to face them with Ben by my side.

And so, I say, "Okay."

* * *

We ask Ben's father's car's GPS to guide us to CityWalk.

"Depart," the GPS says, in the menacing voice of Darth Vader. "Your destiny lies with me."

"What's with the Darth Vader GPS?" I ask Ben as we exit the zoo parking lot.

"When I was a little kid, I put him on there as a joke," Ben says. "My father never took him off."

Darth takes a noisy breath and directs us onto the freeway. My hands sweat as I shift into fourth gear and merge with the speeding traffic. It has been a while since I drove this fast.

I got my driver's license when I was a teenager, but I've never really used it, since I've never owned a car. Honestly, if it hadn't been for Star's dad, I probably wouldn't have bothered getting one at all, and I certainly wouldn't have learned to drive a stick-shift. But when Star's dad was teaching her to drive, she invited me to come along, and he taught me too. He insisted that we learn to drive a stick before he'd let us "be lazy" with an automatic. I really enjoyed those driving lessons with

Star and her dad. He was so enthusiastic and supportive. He made the lessons fun rather than intimidating. Star's parents, like Dylan's and Mateo's, always tried to include me when it came to stuff like that. I haven't spoken to any of them in months. I don't know that they'd want to, now that their children are gone.

"Take the exit right. Do not fail me this time," the GPS says, channeling Darth. "Turn to the right and then proceed as indicated. Don't make me destroy you."

Once I'm off the freeway, I turn onto Lankershim Boulevard and head south, making the first light but missing the next one. I roll to a stop at an intersection with a large church on the corner. The area is abuzz with activity. People mill about on the sidewalk. News reporters talk to their cameras. The sign for the building says, *Saint Charles Borromeo Church.* I recognize that name immediately. An instant later, I remember why.

I point to the church. "That's where they're having the funeral for the girl I found in the ocean."

Ben glances at the time on the car's dashboard. "It's almost five o'clock. Do you want to go to it?"

I spin toward him accusingly. "Did you suggest that we go to CityWalk because you knew we'd pass that church?"

Ben shakes his head. "No."

"So it's a coincidence that we ended up here just in time for the funeral?" I ask, unconvinced.

"Or fate," he says.

"I don't believe in fate."

"I do," Ben says softly.

The traffic light turns green. Behind me, someone taps their car horn. I drive forward, but instead of continuing straight down the road to CityWalk, I pull into the church parking lot.

"Turn around when possible," Darth Vader growls. "I find your lack of faith disturbing."

I silence the protesting GPS and park the car in the first empty space that I see.

And then I sit, staring at the steering wheel, my pulse pounding in my ears.

Chapter Eleven

The inside of the church is packed with slack-faced people mourning a girl I never knew ... at least not in life. Ben and I find a spot to stand against a wall, since there are no unoccupied seats.

A dark-haired woman at the lectern is fighting back tears as she talks about how Alexis volunteered at Children's Hospital Los Angeles every weekend, leading art projects to cheer up the sick kids. The closed coffin behind the woman is covered in sky blue flowers. Beside it, there is a framed photo of a smiling, vivacious girl, but when I look at the coffin, my mind calls up the haunting image of Alexis's bloated, purple, dead body. And then that image is replaced with my last glimpses of Dylan and Mateo and Star, playing in rapid succession, like a terrible slideshow in my mind.

My head throbs with every beat of my accelerating heart. My breaths come fast. My palms go slick with sweat. My legs feel as if they can no longer support my weight. I look for an escape route, but there are people blocking every exit.

I am trapped.

I force myself to inhale deeply as I count silently, *One Mississippi, Two Mississippi, Three ...*

I shake my head and try again.

One Mississippi, Two Mississippi ...

Anxiety floods my chest.

One Mississippi, Two ...

I press my back against the wall and try to focus on the voice of the woman who is speaking, but I can barely keep myself upright.

I can't stay here.

I CAN'T BREATHE!

"I need to get some air," I whisper to Ben.

"I'll come with you," he says.

"Please don't," I say without looking at him. I don't want him to see the panic in my tear-flooded eyes.

I murmur apologies as I clumsily dodge the bodies in my path, my anxiety building when they don't move out of the way quickly enough. Finally, I heave open a heavy door and rush into a deserted corridor.

Instinctively, I head toward the nearest exit, but then I realize that I can't go outside like this. Not with all the cameras and news people out there. I need to go somewhere where I can be alone.

I find a ladies' room, lock myself inside a stall, and sit on the toilet. Then I press my fingers hard against my temples, trying to stop the pounding in my head.

* * *

I feel like I've been in the restroom stall for hours, but I'm sure only minutes have passed. Even though my heart is beating more calmly and my tears have stopped, I don't feel ready to leave. But I need to go back to Ben. I don't want him to worry about me. I open the stall to exit, but I stop short, all of the air suddenly choked from my lungs …

Standing at a sink, looking at me via my reflection in the mirror, tears dripping down her face, is *Alexis*. Of course she isn't actually here. Alexis is dead. I must be imagining her, the same way I imagined seeing Star in the ocean. But this is different. What I see before me now isn't a memory of something I saw in the past. I never knew Alexis when she was alive.

Maybe I'm losing my mind.

"Alexis?" I whisper in my throat.

The girl looks pained, as if I just punched her in the heart.

"I'm Diana," she says. "I'm Alexis's sister. We're ... twins."

Air returns to my lungs.

"I'm so very sorry for your loss," I stammer. That's what people usually say to me when they find out my friends died. I know those words offer little comfort, but I don't know what else to say to her. I wish I could offer something that would bring her a bit of peace, but when people you love die before they truly had a chance to live, there is no peace. Or if there is, I haven't found it.

I wash my hands and then dry them with a paper towel.

"I guess you didn't know her," Diana says to me.

"I was swimming in the ocean on the day she was found," I say.

"Do you know the girl who found her?" she asks.

"I was the girl who found her," I admit.

Diana's eyes search my face for a long time before she speaks again, her voice unsteady, "Someone on social media said she looked terrible."

I recall Alexis's swollen face, opaque eyes, and matted hair. By the time I saw her that day in the ocean, death had ravaged her. She *did* look terrible. But I won't say that to her sister. I want to spare her. And so I shake my head.

I think I see the pain in her eyes lessen a little. "If it wasn't for you, my sister might still be out there ... all alone. I don't think I could have lived with that. Thank you for finding her."

And then Diana wraps me in an embrace. I don't say anything. It feels like, in this moment, words have no place. I hold her until she releases me. When she does, both of us have eyes filled with tears.

"Take care," Diana says softly.

"You too," I whisper back.

And then I give her a small nod. And I go.

When I reenter the church corridor, it doesn't seem like the same place I left just minutes ago. It is now completely packed with people. Too many people in a corridor much too tiny to hold them all. Panic rises inside me. I need to find Ben, but I'm not sure where he is in all this, and the overwhelming tide of people is forcing me in the opposite direction than the one I think I need to go. I feel as if I'm stuck beneath the surface of a tumultuous ocean, unable to breathe. I press myself against the nearest wall, trying to find air there, but I can't seem to find any at all. My head feels light and dizzy. I close my eyes, and I try to make my body go numb. Unfeeling.

Dead.

And then, Ben's hand grips my shoulder. Somehow I feel it through the numbness. He urges me forward, and I blindly take the smallest of steps. There are people in our path, but instead of blocking the way, they move aside and allow us to pass, as if they understand my urgent need to escape.

I don't breathe until sunlight spreads across my face.

When I open my eyes, I see that I am standing just outside the church. Ben's hand still rests on my shoulder, ready to catch me if I fall. I turn my tear-drenched face toward him, finally feeling brave enough to allow him to see how truly broken I am.

Ben looks at me without any noticeable change in his expression. What he sees doesn't seem to surprise him. It's as if he already knew exactly what I've been hiding inside me. It's as if he understands.

Maybe he does.

* * *

The last time I was at CityWalk, the tremendous gleaming silver globe in the misty fountain at the entrance looked welcoming. Now it looks foreboding.

"What are you in the mood for?" Ben asks me, his tone subdued.

"I'd like to go to Saddle Ranch Chop House," I say.

He nods. "Their burgers are great."

"I want to ride their mechanical bull," I say.

Ben's forehead wrinkles. "I didn't think you were the mechanical-bull-riding type."

"I'm not."

"Then why …?" he starts.

I haven't told Ben the reason I decided to make this trip to Los Angeles. I think maybe it's time.

"When I was in high school, I took a trip to L.A. with Dylan, Star, and Mateo. It was one of the highlights of our lives. That's why I came back here. I wanted to relive some of our memories." I take a breath and continue, "Riding that bull was something Star wanted me to do during our trip, but I didn't. I feel like I need to do it now. For her."

"Okay," Ben says softly.

A perky man in jeans and a Saddle Ranch t-shirt greets us at the restaurant entrance. "Here for dinner?" he asks.

"I want to ride the bull first." *I want to do it before I change my mind.*

"Sure," he says with a smile. "Head on back."

As the bull comes into view, I have second—and third—thoughts about doing this, but I push them aside and approach the ring.

"I want to ride," I tell the man who is operating the bull.

He passes me a waiver form on a clipboard. I don't bother reading it. It doesn't matter what it says. I'm going to sign it no matter what. I hand the signed paper back to him, and the man leads me onto the bouncy mats surrounding a padded thing that loosely resembles a bull. I remember watching Star ride this thing. The "bull" shook and bucked and threw her in all different directions for a full minute, but she never fell off. She wouldn't let go.

"That was so fun!" Star said to me afterward, breathless and bursting with adrenaline. "You've gotta try it!"

"I just ate," I said. "I don't want to vomit." That was just an excuse, and Star knew it.

"If you don't want to do it, just say so," she said.

"I *do* want to do it," I said. "But I don't want to look ridiculous." That was the truth.

Star took both of my hands in hers. "If you really want to do something, don't let anyone or anything stop you."

I shook my head. "Maybe next time."

"What if there isn't a next time?" she asked.

"I'm sure there will be," I said.

But I was wrong. There will never be a next time for Star and me.

I take a breath and mount the bull.

"Keep one hand in the air," the operator says. "Have a good time!"

People begin to clap and hoot for me. I search among them, looking for Ben. Finally, I spot him standing quietly, apart from the boisterous onlookers. I hold his gaze ... and then the bull whips me around in a circle, instantly disorienting me.

I grip onto the bull with my right hand and my legs. The bull bucks forward and back. I cling to him as the crowd roars. I force my ears to go deaf, silencing the world so I can concentrate solely on riding. The bull shakes. He dips. He spins. Violently. So violently. I feel myself slipping. Falling. I could let myself fall. If I fall, this will all be over. But that's the easy way out. Star wouldn't have approved. In the entire time I knew her, she only took the easy way out once.

The bull tries again and again to throw me to the ground, but I fight. I struggle with everything in me to stay on top of that bull. I fight as if my life depends on it ...

And then the bull slows to a stop.

Cheers break through the silence in my head.

The world comes back into focus.

The bull operator runs up to me and offers his hand. "Great job!" he shouts.

My arms and legs trembling, I slide down off the bull.

Shakily, I walk to the ring exit. Ben meets me there.

"You did the entire minute!" he gushes. "Let's get some dinner and celebrate!"

"Can we just ... go?" I ask.

"Go where?" he asks.

"Anywhere," I say.

Ben swallows. "All right."

By the time we get into the car, I'm crying. I close the door and drop my face into my hands.

"I'm sorry, Ben," I say. "You just wanted to have a nice dinner—"

He shakes his head. "I don't care about eating. I could go all night without eating."

My tears stop at Ben's selflessness.

"Did the bull hurt you?" he asks me.

"No," I say. "Just the opposite. Riding that bull made me feel stronger. Stronger than I've felt in such a long time."

Ben reaches up and gently strokes my cheek, wiping

away my tears. I close my eyes and allow myself to experience the warmth of his fingers on my face. But Ben's touch isn't just comforting. It reignites a feeling deep inside me. I want to kiss Ben. And I am all but certain that he wants to kiss me too.

I am disappointed when he withdraws his hand.

"What is it?" he asks, maybe sensing my disappointment.

"I'm starving," I say, afraid to tell him the truth.

"I know a great Italian place," he suggests.

I nod. "Okay."

* * *

It is as if Ben and I have traveled to old-world Italy. The murals covering the inner walls of Miceli's restaurant make me feel like we're outdoors in a charming Italian neighborhood. We sit in a cozy booth near a pianist, whose fingers dance over black and white keys, playing vaguely familiar music. *Star would have loved this place.*

A waiter took our order a few minutes ago. We're getting the veggie pizza, which Ben said has been his favorite dish here ever since he was a little kid. Our waiter pops into the kitchen then returns empty handed and picks up a microphone. At first, I wonder if he is going to make some sort of announcement, but then the pianist starts a new song, and the waiter begins *to sing.* Another waiter grabs a second microphone and joins him in a duet about the obstacles that fairy-tale princes face when pursuing love. I watch delightedly as the two men stroll around the restaurant, serenading our fellow diners: an elderly woman who nods her head in time to the music, a shy little girl who hides behind her menu, an older man who joins the waiters in singing a few lines. The final note of the song is met by enthusiastic applause, and then our waiter hurries back into the kitchen and returns with our dinner.

As I bite into a slice of pizza, two waitresses step up to the piano and begin a poignant song about people who changed one another's lives. As the women sing, I can't help reflecting on my own life. There are many people who have altered my life—both in small ways and in big ones, in good ways and in bad ones. But, ultimately, the people who changed my life the most have left painful scars on my heart, scars that I will carry with me forever.

I can't help wondering if Ben will leave one there too.

* * *

After dinner, Ben and I encounter extraordinarily thick traffic on the way back to his house.

"Will you be joining me again tomorrow?" I ask Ben as I inch the car along.

He smiles. "What will we be doing?"

When I initially planned this trip, I had my final day in Los Angeles all figured out. I was going to visit the charming little Mexican shops of Olvera Street. At lunchtime, I'd pop over to Chinatown for dim sum. After spending the afternoon wandering around downtown, I'd stop for a dinner of ramen noodles in Little Tokyo. That was how my friends and I spent our final day in Los Angeles. But now, I wonder if I should spend my last day here making new memories instead of trying to relive old ones.

"If you had only one day to spend in L.A., how would you spend it?" I ask Ben.

He thinks for a moment, and then he says, "I'd go for a hike in Malibu Creek State Park. That's where they filmed the TV show *M*A*S*H* and the original *Planet of the Apes* movie."

"That sounds cool," I say.

He goes on, "Then I'd go to Point Dume Beach. There are tide pools there with anemones and starfish as big as your hand."

"Wow," I say.

But Ben isn't done. "I'd finish the night at Griffith

Observatory, where I'd take a look through the Zeiss telescope on the roof."

Suddenly, I can't imagine spending my final day in Los Angeles any other way.

"That's what I want to do tomorrow," I say.

We round a bend, and the traffic thickens even more than before.

"Looks like there's a show at the Bowl tonight," Ben says.

"A show at the *what*?" I ask.

"The Hollywood Bowl," he says. "It's a stadium where they have concerts. I wonder who's performing."

Several minutes later, I see a sign. "John Williams, Maestro of the Movies, Tonight 8 PM," I read.

"Williams' music is epic!" Ben says. "He wrote the scores for *Star Wars* and *Harry Potter* and tons of other films! You want to go to the concert?"

I smile. "Let's go."

* * *

According to the apologetic woman at the ticket counter, there are about ten thousand seats in the Hollywood Bowl, but tonight's performance was completely sold out … until she refreshed her computer screen one last time, and two tickets became available.

Our seats are in the uppermost tier of the colossal arena, practically the furthest seats from the stage, but we have a spectacular view of the surrounding mountains. Ben and I admire the view until the sky darkens and the conductor takes the stage. He's so far away that he appears to be just a few millimeters tall. We stand and place our hands over our hearts as he conducts the miniature orchestra playing "The Star-Spangled Banner."

After we settle back into our seats, music begins that I recognize instantly—thanks to numerous *Harry Potter* movie marathons with my best friends. As I listen contentedly, I gaze up at the blanket of glittering stars above us and imagine that I am sitting in a gigantic Great Hall, with an enchanted nighttime sky for a ceiling. As a small child, I used to wish I had magic powers. I'd thought that would make my life easy, but now I realize that magic alone is far from enough to survive in this world.

I glance over at Ben and discover that he is looking at me. My heart quickens as I notice the unmistakable longing in his eyes. I feel it too. Suddenly, I am absolutely desperate to kiss him. It feels as if I have no choice. It's as if gravity has shifted and is driving us together. Our bodies grow closer and closer until our faces are only inches apart. I close my eyes, surrendering to whatever is about to happen, certain that I am unable to stop it, knowing that I don't want to stop it. I want to kiss Ben more than I want to breathe.

But then applause thunders around us, shifting gravity back the way it was before.

Ben and I pull apart.

The moment is gone.

* * *

After the concert, complete with two encores, Ben and I cascade out of the Hollywood Bowl, riding the wave of people. We find our car buried inside the parking lot, completely boxed in.

"It doesn't look like we're getting out of here anytime soon," Ben says.

That fact doesn't bother me. The idea of sitting in the car with Ben, stuck in the middle of a parking lot, feels exciting rather than terrifying. We unlock the car and climb inside to wait until the other concertgoers arrive to move their cars.

"That was a great concert," Ben says.

"Yes," I say. "It was."

And then I turn toward him, and my body stills at the intensity of his gaze. His hand rises to my face and touches my cheek, very hesitantly at first, then more forcefully. His thumb moves down to my lips and brushes against them. My chest aches with desire. My heart races with anticipation. I want to kiss Ben so desperately now that it's more of a *need* than a *want* …

Abruptly, he withdraws his hand and rubs his forehead.

"What's wrong?" I ask, concerned.

He leans back against his seat and closes his eyes. "Nothing."

I force away the questions that flood my brain. I have so many, but it doesn't feel right to ask any of them. Clearly, for whatever reason, Ben doesn't want us to kiss. And so we won't. I exhale and lean back against my own seat, willing myself not to feel all the feelings inside me.

After quiet minutes that stretch on like hours, someone honks their car horn. The cars that were boxing us in are gone. Now ours is the only one blocking the way.

I press the ignition button, and the car comes to life.

I fasten my seatbelt, and Ben fastens his.

And then I ask the GPS to guide us home.

We travel all the way back to Ben's house in silence.

Except for the menacing voice of Darth Vader.

Chapter Twelve

I awaken to a scratching sound coming from outside Ben's guest room door. In the hallway, I find Bolt. As I lean down to pet the soft fur behind his ears, I notice the muted clicking of the keys of Ben's laptop. I walk over to his open doorway and smile when I see him typing just as intently as he was yesterday.

Rather than disturb him, I go to the kitchen. The TV is on, but I barely pay attention to it as I prepare my almond butter and granola breakfast. I'm almost finished eating when Ben comes into the room and fills a glass with water.

"We should probably get going," he says. "We've got a lot to do today."

I swallow my surprise. After our silent drive home last night, I didn't think Ben would want to spend today together, but apparently he does.

"Right," I say, rising from my seat. "I'll go finish getting ready."

I stuff my last bite of breakfast into my mouth and bring my dishes to the sink without making eye contact with him. Today could prove to be the most uncomfortable day ever.

I might end up regretting spending my final day in L.A. with Ben.

But I know I will regret it if I don't.

* * *

Our hike in Malibu Creek State Park begins in rolling meadows. Then we follow a trail that meanders past a duck-inhabited creek before it veers off and makes its way into a pine forest. After we cross a stream, we amble along a boulder-strewn trail that deposits us in a valley surrounded by rocky hills.

Ben and I didn't talk much on our drive this morning, and we haven't really conversed during our hike, but the silence has felt soothing rather than awkward. Maybe, right now, just being together is enough.

As we round a bend, Ben points out an old-fashioned army ambulance parked in a patch of dry grass and announces, "We made it to the *M*A*S*H* site."

The ambulance looks freshly painted, appearing ready for its next patient but, when I walk over to it and peer inside, its rusted-out interior reveals the truth. The ambulance is a mere shell of what it once was.

Ben and I continue along the dirt trail, where we find two more vehicles. Unlike the first one, these are thoroughly rusted both inside and out. In a former life, one might have been an ambulance. The other, probably a jeep.

Ben leads me to some plaques that display screenshots from the *M*A*S*H* TV show. I compare the images from the past to what I see in the present. Other than the fact that the elaborate TV show sets are gone, little has changed over the years. The towering hills that were their backdrop look more or less the same.

Once we have visited every plaque, Ben points to a steep trail. "Let's go up there."

I follow him up the trail to a flat area covered in twisted shrubs.

"On *M*A*S*H*, this was the helicopter landing area," Ben explains.

I don't think I ever saw the TV show, and there are no plaques here, but in my mind I picture a green army helicopter swooping majestically out of the blue cloudless sky to land here.

Ben holds out his hand to me. "Would you like to dance?"

I'm not sure why Ben wants to dance with me here, but I accept his hand. He places his other hand on my hip and begins to hum a melancholy tune that I don't recognize.

"What song is that?" I ask.

"It's the *M*A*S*H* theme song," Ben says. "It's called 'Suicide is Painless.'"

I wince. "That's a terrible name for a song."

"Yeah." Ben nods. Then he starts humming it again.

And we dance. To "Suicide is Painless."

* * *

In a valley of craggy hills—about a one-hour hike away from the *M*A*S*H* filming site—Ben and I settle down on a large rock at the edge of a mirrored pond that Ben calls "*Planet of the Apes* Lake," because it's where they filmed some of the scenes for that movie.

Planet of the Apes was one of Mateo's favorite movies. He tried to get Dylan, Star, and me to watch it with him multiple times, but we always ended up watching something else. I wish Mateo could have seen this place in person. If we'd come here, he probably would have leapt right into the center of the pond and single-handedly acted out every one of the movie scenes that was filmed here from memory.

I miss Mateo and his antics. He was the brother I always wanted but never got. And I miss Star and her kindness. She was the big sister I desperately needed. And I miss Dylan and the way he loved me. Dylan, Star, and Mateo were three of the best people I've ever met. It isn't right that they died so young. I would give anything to change that, even trade my life for theirs. To be honest, I wish I could.

Fiercely, I wipe away my tears.

"What wrong?" Ben asks.

"I hate that I'm here, and Dylan, Star, and Mateo aren't," I say.

"It's not your fault that you survived," Ben says gently.

"We were celebrating *my* birthday that night," I say. "They were in that limo … because of me."

"They died because of an accident," Ben counters. "Not because of you."

I shake my head. "Dylan and Mateo died from the accident. But Star and I were sent home from the hospital. We were both supposed to make a full recovery. I could have saved Star … but I didn't."

Ben's forehead furrows. "How did she die?"

"After the night of the accident, Star and I didn't really talk to each other. She said she needed space to process things, so I gave her space. Honestly, even if she'd wanted to talk, I'm not sure if I could have. Some days I barely got out of bed. Eating and drinking took almost more effort than I could muster. I would just look at old photos of my friends, and I'd cry.

"One Saturday morning, I felt like I really needed Star. I needed my friend back. So I forced myself out of bed, and I took a bus to her parent's house, where she was staying to recuperate. Star's parents spent Saturdays volunteering at a food bank, so I thought it would be a good chance to talk to her alone.

"When I got to her house, I heard a car running in the garage, but the door was closed. I knew the security code from back when we were kids, so I used it to open the door." I take a breath, trying to find the strength to continue. "Star was sitting in her dad's car. Her eyes were open, but there wasn't any life in them. She died from intentional carbon monoxide poisoning."

"She didn't want anyone to save her," Ben says softly.

I look at him through wet eyes. "How do you know?"

"The day that I went to my father's office to end my life was a *Sunday*. I planned it that way, because I knew no one would be in the office until Monday, when my father came in to work. By then I would be long dead. I didn't know there was a janitor who came in over the weekends. That's the only reason I survived. Because of the janitor."

Sadness rises into my throat. "So you didn't want to be saved either?"

"I thought there was nothing good left for me in life. I was sure of that," he says. "But I was wrong. I realize that now. Life isn't fair, and it isn't always good, but it *is* worth living."

I rest my head on Ben's shoulder, and he puts his arm around me and draws me close in a way that makes me profoundly aware of the bond between us. A bond so powerful that I feel like I can almost touch it. A bond so strong that it feels as if nothing can sever it.

I can't imagine Ben ever letting me go.

Chapter Thirteen

I drive along a narrow road flanked by a rocky hillside and a white-sand beach. Darth informed Ben and me that we arrived at our destination a few minutes ago. Now he is vehemently insisting that we turn back. But Ben tells me to keep driving, so I silence Darth and drive until Ben tells me to stop.

Once on foot, we follow a rugged cliffside trail that rises and then descends before it finally ends at a rusted metal staircase. The staircase leads us down to the tide pools at Point Dume Beach, the ones Ben told me yesterday that he wanted to visit.

We spend the next hour going from tide pool to tide pool, admiring anemones, large and small. And there are starfish as big as our hands. Yellow ones, pink ones, and purple ones. And tons of hermit crabs. The pools are mesmerizing, but I can tell that Ben's heart isn't into this. Something is troubling him, and I'm not sure if I should ask what it is. After his response to my question in the car last night, I have a feeling that asking him won't help. I think I need to wait for him to tell me. But I don't know if he will.

As the sun begins to sink toward the horizon, Ben and I make our way back up to the top of the cliff to find a spot to sit and watch the sunset.

For a while, we don't speak.

Then Ben says, "It's going to be hard to say goodbye to you."

His words hit me like a blow to the chest, knocking all of the air from my lungs. Strangely, up until this moment, I hadn't really thought about saying goodbye to Ben. I suppose I was so focused on the present that I hadn't considered the future. I think, if I had, I wouldn't have been able to bond with Ben the way I did.

And I desperately needed to bond with Ben. I don't think I could have survived the emptiness of being alone for even one day more. I needed to connect with someone in order to carry on. The problem is, now that I've gotten to know Ben, I don't just need *someone*. I need *him*.

Ben slides his hand into mine, and I cling to it as the

fiery sliver of sun fades into the ocean.

When the sun slips below the horizon, he finally turns toward me.

And both of our faces are streaked with tears.

* * *

It takes almost two hours to drive back to Hollywood from Malibu. Ben and I fill the time with quiet small talk, occasionally interrupted by Darth's breathy directions.

We are almost at Ben's street when he asks me, "Still up for the observatory?"

The observatory was on our itinerary for today, but I thought, after our tear-filled sunset, that maybe our plans had changed. I guess they haven't.

"Okay," I say.

I silence Darth. I know the way from here.

* * *

The observatory doesn't feel nearly as claustrophobic as it did the last time I visited, even though there are easily twice as many people here tonight. I suppose it helps that I have Ben by my side.

After taking in some of the exhibits, Ben and I go up to the roof to check out the view through the massive

Zeiss telescope. Together, we climb up the stairs to the eyepiece. Ben peers through it first, but he doesn't tell me what he sees. All he says is, "Have a look."

I gaze through the eyepiece, and I am shocked at how incredibly close I suddenly feel to the moon. I can see little details in its craters: sharp rims, steep walls, and shadowed floors. For the first time in my life, the moon feels real, like someplace that I could walk around on and touch. Of course, I will probably never get to visit the moon, but as I stare through that telescope, it seems possible.

When Ben and I exit the telescope room, I walk to the edge of the observatory roof—toward the distant glittering lights of nighttime Los Angeles—feeling incredibly small, like a tiny sentient speck of dust. How, in this gigantic city, did I find the exact person I needed precisely when I needed him? It can't be a coincidence. Maybe it's fate.

Ben comes up behind me and wraps his arms around me. Instantly, I feel big again, as if the minuscule bit of universe that holds Ben and me suddenly expanded.

And, in that moment, I make a decision.

* * *

I wait until Ben and I are resting side-by-side on the

lounge chairs by his pool, gazing up at the stars, before I say to him, "I decided something tonight."

"What did you decide?" he asks.

I turn toward him. "I'm going to stay in Los Angeles."

Ben stiffens. "No."

For a while, I don't breathe. I lie frozen in place, waiting for an explanation, but he doesn't offer one. I'd expected him to be thrilled. Instead, he seems ... horrified.

"If I stay here, we can be together," I try to explain.

"Erin, we both knew this was only temporary," he says quietly.

I swallow the pain rising in my throat. "Is that what you *wanted*?"

Ben runs his fingers through his hair, avoiding my gaze. "It wasn't supposed to end like this," he says, almost to himself.

"Like what?" I ask.

He shakes his head. "We weren't supposed to fall in love with each other."

"You don't love me," I say bitterly.

"I do," he whispers.

"Then why don't you want me to stay?" I ask.

"Someday you'll understand," he says, still avoiding

my eyes.

"What will I understand?" I ask, confused.

Ben shakes his head again, and I squeeze my eyes shut, forcing back the tears that are begging to come. *I hate Ben.* I hate him for not wanting me to be with him and refusing to tell me why. But, at the same time, I love him. It's not normal—and it's probably insane—to fall in love with someone so fast, but I did. And now, feelings of love and hate are waging an excruciating battle inside me, fighting a war that can't be won. The only way to move on is to let one of those feelings go: the love or the hate. I decide to make the terrifying choice, the dangerous choice, the choice that could destroy me if my decision is the wrong one. But it is the only choice I can live with …

I decide to let go of the hate.

"I'm going to tell you something I wasn't planning to ever tell you," I say.

Ben still doesn't look at me. "Okay."

"When I got back to New York, I was going to take my dad's car and drive to the boat ramp at the pond where Dylan died. Then I was going to swallow a bunch of sleeping pills and drive the car into the water." Ben inhales as if he's about to speak, but before he can say anything, I continue, "I don't want to die anymore. I don't want to die because I love you. I never thought it would be possible for me to feel that way about anyone again. I thought I was too broken. But I'm not. And as long as I'm still capable of loving someone, I want to live."

"Let's go for a swim," Ben says.

Without waiting for a response, he lifts his t-shirt over his head, then he unzips his shorts and pulls them off, leaving him in only his boxers. He looks more vulnerable than I've ever seen him.

I want to be vulnerable with him.

Ben watches as I slowly unbutton my shirt and then slip it off. I slide my shorts off as well. And then I stand facing him, wearing only my underwear.

Ben turns away and dives into the pool, sinking all the way to the bottom. I dive in after him, forcing myself to the bottom as well. We look at each other for a moment, then I grab a breath and take off toward the opposite end of the pool. I swim fast to the wall, and then I stop and twirl around. Ben is right beside me. I race past him, back to the other end of the pool, stopping only for a quick gasp of air. Just before I reach the other side, Ben grabs my ankle. I spin toward him, and he releases his grip as he stares into my eyes. For a moment, I feel as if I could stay right here under the water with Ben.

Forever. But, of course, that's not true.

I push off the bottom of the pool and splash to the surface, gasping for air. Ben surfaces next to me, his breathing ragged. He presses me against the edge of the pool and looks deep into my eyes with an intensity that is indescribable. Yet again, it seems as if he wants to kiss me … and I can't bear the thought of him turning away this time.

"I want to kiss you," I breathe.

"Why?" he asks.

I inhale and speak with my heart rather than my head. "Because I can't imagine *never* kissing you."

Ben's eyes flash with pain. "I don't want to make tomorrow any harder than it's already going to be."

I shake my head. "I don't think that's possible."

The muscles in Ben's jaw tense.

My pulse pounds.

He swallows. "You're probably right."

And then, almost involuntarily, Ben and I kiss. The way his lips meet mine is extraordinarily gentle, yet unbelievably fierce. Waves of warm energy surge between us, rising and falling. My heart aches and soars as every cell in my body focuses on being with Ben. I feel him take absolutely everything from me, and yet he leaves me full rather than empty.

After our kiss, we just hold each other, our bodies quiet and still …

Except for the pounding of our hearts.

Chapter Fourteen

I wake up where I fell asleep: in Ben's bed. I remember lying beside him last night, trying desperately to stay awake so I could experience every remaining moment we had together. But my eyelids became heavier and heavier. I finally had to shut them, just to rest them for a few minutes. That's the last thing I recall until now.

Ben's laptop sits closed on his desk. Before we got into bed, he finally showed me his screenplay. It isn't finished, of course, but he has made substantial progress. It is, as I'd suggested, inspired by a true story. The story of a boy who meets a girl in a coffee shop. Ben wouldn't tell me how it ends. Maybe that's because he doesn't know yet.

I hug Ben's pillow and inhale the clean, sweet scent that is only his, then I climb out of bed. Bolt comes running to greet me, purring enthusiastically when I pet him.

"Where's Ben?" I ask Bolt.

The TV chatters away in the kitchen. I go there, expecting to find Ben waiting for me. But he isn't in the kitchen. I walk back down the hallway, checking each room, but I don't see Ben in any of them.

I listen for signs of life upstairs. Hearing none, I call up the stairway, "Ben?"

There's no answer.

I run upstairs and poke my head into every doorway, calling Ben's name, but I get no response.

I go back downstairs and into the backyard. "Ben?"

I check the hot tub and the pool. "Ben?"

In a few hours, I'll be getting on an airplane headed back to New York. *Why would Ben leave me alone in my final hours here?* He must have run out to do an errand or something. I hope he isn't gone long. I was thinking we could go have a final cup of coffee this morning at the shop where we met …

But maybe that would be too heartbreaking.

I walk back to Ben's room and sit down at his desk. While I'm waiting for him, maybe I can upload the photos on my camera to Ben's laptop, that way he'll have copies in case he ever wants to look at them.

When I turn on the laptop, a password screen comes up.

I try the only password I can think of: bolt.

That is incorrect.

I highlight the "b" and change it to "B."

I'm in!

I retrieve my camera and connect it to the laptop. My photos appear on the screen as tiny thumbnails. I select them all and drop them into a new folder that I name "Ben and Erin." Then I click "Slide show."

The first photo fills the screen: celebrity hand and footprints. It's blurry. *I don't remember taking that one.* The next one is me with the footprints. It's the one taken by the Japanese tourist. But Ben is missing from the photo. He must have stepped away at the last moment so he wouldn't be in the picture. *But why would he do that?* The next photo is a selfie I took during our hike to the Hollywood Sign. The photo shows just me, not Ben, even though I'd thought he was right next to me when I took the picture.

I look at photo after photo. Not one of them includes Ben.

He must have been deliberately trying to avoid having his picture taken.

I go to the living room. To the framed photos on the

mantle. I'd noticed them before, but I hadn't looked at them. Now, I study them. Ben is in every picture: little Ben in a cap and gown graduating from preschool, young Ben at the top of a slide at a playground, slightly older Ben riding a horse. There's a professional portrait of teenage Ben with a smiling man and woman. They must be his parents. I stare at the eyes of the man. *He doesn't look like a monster.* But monsters don't always look like monsters.

I grab a photo that looks recent. Of Ben standing alone in front of Griffith Observatory. Stuffing it into my backpack, I sprint out the door and race the few blocks to the coffee shop. Then I compose myself and go inside.

I scan the tables. I don't see Ben.

At the counter, the same girl who was working here on my other visits greets me.

"Erin, right?" she asks.

I nod.

"What can I get for you?" she asks.

I reach into my backpack, pull out the framed photo of Ben, and say, "I'm looking for this guy."

She smiles. "Ben."

"Yeah," I say. "Has he been in here today?"

"How did you know him?" she asks without answering.

I freeze at her words. "Why did you say '*did*'?"

"Ben died three months ago," she says softly.

My heart nearly stops. "No, he can't be dead."

"He died of complications from leukemia," she says.

My voice barely comes. "How do you know that?"

She swallows. "I went to his funeral."

I feel as if I'm going to pass out. I step away from the counter and sit at the table where I once sat with Ben. I am numb and empty. Lost and confused.

And yet, now everything makes sense ...

These past few days, I was the only one who felt Ben's presence.

Ben impacted only me, nothing and no one else.

Looking back, there were signs, but I hadn't allowed myself to see them.

I had accepted with my entire heart and soul that Ben was here with me. But he wasn't.

Ben is dead. Just like Dylan and Mateo and Star.

It's not possible to see him or hear him or touch him. Or kiss him.

But, somehow, I did.

* * *

Nothing has changed in the universe. Ben was dead when I "met" him. Still, I mourn my loss. The only way

153

to close the distance between us is for me to die. And I no longer want to die.

Bolt follows me through the house as I return Ben's photo to the mantle and then go back to Ben's bedroom and delete the "Ben and Erin" folder from his laptop. I am about to shut the laptop down when an icon on the homepage catches my eye. It is for a document labeled simply, "Screenplay."

My heart pounds as I click on it.

It takes a full minute for the document to open but, finally, it does. On the first page, I read, "Untitled Screenplay by Benjamin Weston." I attempt to scroll down, but there is nothing more. The document is only a single page long. Ben's screenplay was never written. Just like his life, it was left unfinished. Like Dylan, Mateo, and Star, Ben was taken from the world far too soon.

I shut down Ben's laptop and gently close it. Then I go back to the guest room, where I pack my belongings and straighten up, endeavoring to leave no trace of my visit. When I go to turn off the still-chattering TV in the kitchen, I notice something by the plug: a timer. *The TV will turn itself off, and it will turn itself on again tomorrow.* I don't disturb it. I check Bolt's food and water dishes in the alcove and discover that they are automated. There is a note taped above them thanking someone named Mary—the cat sitter, I assume—for checking in on him. I guess it's lucky that Mary and I never crossed paths.

On my way out of the house, I stop by the mantle one last time. For a moment, I consider whether Ben's mom would miss that photo of Ben at the observatory. But I don't take it. It isn't mine to take. Instead, I pull out my camera and snap a picture of the photo. It's the closest thing to a picture of Ben that I will ever have.

As I slip my camera back into its case, a photo on a small table beside the mantle catches my eye. The frame is made of shells glued to wooden popsicle sticks, like something a small child might make as a craft project. I pick it up, and I'm forced to sit on the floor because my legs have gone limp. The photo is of two women and two children on a beach. The first woman has long brown hair. I recognize her, even though I don't remember knowing her. She is wearing a flowery purple dress with white lace trim. It is the exact same dress she is wearing in one of the few photos I have of her. *The woman is my mother.* Nestled in her lap is a tiny version of me—about three years old—wearing a matching dress. Next to us is Ben's mom. On her lap is an adorable little Ben. Ben and I are holding hands and smiling broad smiles. I stare at our small hands. Touching.

I'm not sure whether the Ben I knew over the past few days was an angel, or a ghost, or some kind of hallucination. But this photo is real.

Long before he died, Ben and I knew each other.

We once held hands.

I carefully aim my camera—wishing I could stop my hands from trembling—and take a picture of the photo. Then I kiss Bolt goodbye, hide the spare house key in the squirrel statue, and go sit on the curb with my suitcase to wait for the airport shuttle. The shuttle isn't supposed to come for another hour, but I don't want to stay in Ben's home any longer without him.

* * *

About half an hour after I sit down on the curb, a town car pulls up. I wonder if the shuttle company made a mistake and sent a town car for me instead of a van ... until the back door opens and Ben's mom climbs out. The driver retrieves two large suitcases from the trunk and carefully sets them down on the sidewalk. Ben's mom tips him and then heads toward the house, wheeling the suitcases behind her.

I stand and hear myself say, "Excuse me, ma'am. I'm Erin Winters." I'm not sure if she will recognize my name, but it is the only thing I can think of to say.

Ben's mom turns and looks at me for what feels like an eternity. Then she abandons her bags on the walkway, rushes over, and throws her arms around me.

She hugs me tightly and then pulls away and stares at me in disbelief for a moment before she asks, "How did you find me?"

"It's a long story, and I only have a few minutes before my airport shuttle gets here," I say.

Even if I did have time to tell her the whole story, I'm not sure how I could possibly tell it without sounding completely insane.

She gestures toward the front door of the house. "Please come inside."

I don't remember ever using the front door of Ben's house. These past few days, I only used the side door. But, as I stand before the distinctive door, with its faint images of forest animals carved into the wood, I feel a twinge of déjà vu. I suddenly wonder if this isn't the first time I've entered Ben's house through this door.

"Have I been to this house before?" I ask Ben's mom as she unlocks the door.

She nods. "Yes, with your mom, when you were a little girl."

As the door opens, Bolt comes running, his collar

jingling. Ben's mom scoops him into her arms and lovingly kisses him on the head before setting him back down again.

"Make yourself at home," Ben's mom says to me, motioning to the couch.

After the two of us settle down there, I take a breath and ask her, "How well did you know my mother?"

She smiles wistfully. "We met on our first day of junior high school, and we were best friends from that day on."

Hope floods into my heart. I think of all the questions that have haunted me for as long as I can remember. If Ben's mom and my mother were best friends, she might know the answers.

I start, "My mother left me and my father when I was very little—"

Her face falls. "I know."

"Do you know *why* she left us?" I ask.

She exhales. "I'm not sure."

"But you have an idea," I say, sensing that from her answer.

"Your mother loved you very much, but she had a restless soul. She dreamed of traveling the world. I think maybe that's what she did."

"Do you know where she might be now?" I ask.

She shakes her head. "I tried to find her many times, but my searches always came up empty."

I exhale every shred of hope I was holding onto. For a moment, I'd allowed myself to believe that Ben's mom would have the answer to my most important question. But she doesn't.

"I really don't remember my mother at all," I admit. "I wish I knew more about her."

Ben's mom rises from the couch. "I'll be right back."

She hurries off and returns with a thick photo album that has a map of the world on the cover. She places the album on my lap and opens it. On the first page are photos of Ben's mom and my mom as young teenagers at a beach. They look so … happy.

I turn the pages, drinking in the images of birthdays, holidays, hanging out, and clowning around. Then there are pictures of my mom and Ben's mom lounging on the lawn of Griffith Observatory, and posing with the Hollywood Sign, and standing on a footbridge that arches over a canal. Beside the canal photo, there is a picture of the girls with a gray-haired woman. They are standing in front of the same mural I stumbled on in Venice a few days ago, the mural that I'd thought at first glance featured Star and me.

I point to the photo, and Ben's mom explains, "Your mother and I took a trip to L.A. when we were seniors in high school. That woman said we were so cute that she couldn't resist painting us into her work of art."

For a few moments, I stare at the photo of the mural, wondering if I now know why I was so drawn to it when I saw it in person. Then I pour over the rest of the pictures from my mom's trip to Los Angeles with her best friend. In every photo, both girls' eyes are filled with excitement, and their smiles are unrestrained. I am struck by how much they remind me of Star and me.

A few birthdays and holidays later, there is a photo of Ben's mom and my mom sitting on a bench in a park, each with a tiny baby in their arms.

"Is that me?" I ask, pointing at the infant in my mom's arms.

"Yes," Ben's mom says, then she points to the other infant. "And that's my son, Ben. You two were inseparable."

The photos that follow document the life Ben and I once shared. I see baby Ben and me fast asleep, side-by-side in a playpen. And hugging an enormous pumpkin. And riding on a sled in the snow. Page after page, as I watch us grow into best friends, I see the light fade from my mom's eyes, and her smile becomes weary. After a while, my mom disappears from the photos. Maybe she didn't have the energy to force a smile any longer.

The final photo in the book shows toddler Ben giving me a huge hug as I grin delightedly. I can't stop looking at that photo.

"He loved you," Ben's mom says. "I wish you and Ben could get to know each other again. But he passed away a few months ago."

Even though I already knew this, her words shatter my heart. It's as if looking at these photos brought Ben back to life. Now, the truth sends me plummeting back into reality.

"Do you remember him?" Ben's mom asks.

I don't consciously remember knowing Ben back when we were children, but I am certain that, deep down inside, some part of me *does* remember him. Maybe that explains how I ended up here. Maybe my subconscious memories guided me to exactly where I am now. Either way, I know that I loved Ben then, and I still do. That is why it hurts so much to have lost him. And I know that, despite the scar he has left on my heart, my life is better for having had him in it, even if he couldn't stay in it forever. Like Dylan, Star, and Mateo, Ben helped make me stronger …

Strong enough to survive.

"I will *never* forget him," I whisper.

I didn't cry when I found out Ben was dead. Now, I sob so hard that my whole body shakes. Ben's mom takes me in her arms, crying too.

And then my phone beeps.

"My shuttle is here," I tell Ben's mom, trying to dry my tears.

"Hold on."

She dashes off again. An instant later, she returns with a thin book titled "Ben and Erin." On the cover is the same photo of Ben, me, and our moms that sits on the small table beside the mantle.

"I made this for Ben when he was little," she says. "He'd want you to have it."

"Thank you," I say, my eyes filling with tears again.

She scribbles something on a piece of paper and hands it to me. "Here's my phone number and email address. Please keep in touch, Erin."

"I will," I say.

And then she wraps me in one final embrace.

It takes every last bit of my strength to let her go.

* * *

I wait until I'm safely ensconced in my cramped airline seat and my seatmate has drifted off to sleep before I remove Ben's book from my backpack and open it. Inside the front cover is a sticker that says "This book belongs to" with a line under it. On the line, in big blue crayon letters, is scrawled "Ben," with a backward "B." I smile, imagining little Ben carefully printing his name in the book.

I turn to the first page, and my jaw goes slack. The page is filled with a collage of more than a dozen pictures of Ben and me when we were young children. Among them, I spot us posing with big smiles at the entrance of the Los Angeles Zoo, eating slices of veggie pizza at Miceli's Restaurant, balancing on top of a large rock at the edge of *Planet of the Apes* Lake, and comparing our little feet to Harrison Ford's footprints in the cement in front of the fancy movie theater in Hollywood. All of these places that I'd thought I was visiting for the first time during this trip, I actually visited before … with Ben … a long time ago.

I swallow the lump in my throat, and I read:

Ben and Erin:
The Tale of Two Forever Friends
By Mommy

Ben and Erin were born on the very same day,

in the very same hospital,
in the very same room.

Their mommies were best friends.
Ben and Erin were best friends too.

Ben and Erin visited each other almost every day.
They went for walks in Central Park,
and to see the stars at Hayden Planetarium,
and to play in the waves at Jones Beach.

They had many, many, many adventures together.

One day, Ben's family had to move to California.
Ben was sad that Erin couldn't come with him ...
But then Erin came for a visit!

They went for walks in Malibu Creek State Park,
and to explore the tide pools at Point Dume Beach,
and to look through the big telescope at Griffith
Observatory.

They made many, many, many memories.

When it was time for Erin to go home,

Ben and Erin put all of those memories in their hearts,
for safekeeping.
They knew they would see each other again someday.

Because Ben and Erin were forever friends.

The final two words have been scribbled out by firm strokes of blue crayon. They are barely legible:

The End

* * * * *

ALSO BY J.W. LYNNE

IF I TELL
A girl wonders if her father is a serial killer.

ABOVE THE SKY
A girl and boy fall in love in a dangerous world filled
with secrets.

THE UNKNOWN
Eight kids learn the shocking reason why they were
kidnapped.

THE DARKNESS OUTSIDE
Ten families are locked in a bunker to take a simulated
trip to the moon.

WILD ANIMAL SCHOOL
A girl falls in love while spending the summer caring for
elephants, tigers, bears, leopards, and lions at an exotic
animal ranch.

KID DOCS
An experimental program teaches kids to be doctors.

Made in the USA
Monee, IL
04 December 2024

72424932R00100